Francis Muench

Palmetto Lyrics

Francis Muench

Palmetto Lyrics

ISBN/EAN: 9783744784078

Printed in Europe, USA, Canada, Australia, Japan

Cover: Foto ©Andreas Hilbeck / pixelio.de

More available books at **www.hansebooks.com**

EMILY GEIGER.

BY

F. MUENCH, Ph. D.

WITH AN INTRODUCTION,

BY

THE REV. CHARLES S. VEDDER, D. D., LL.D.

1896.

LUCAS & RICHARDSON CO., PUBLISHERS,

CHARLESTON, S. C.

TO

THE BOYS AND GIRLS

OF

THE PALMETTO STATE

THIS LITTLE VOLUME, A LABOR OF LOVE,

IS SINCERELY INSCRIBED BY

THE AUTHOR.

INTRODUCTION.

By the Rev. Charles S. Vedder, D. D., LL.D.

NDREW FLETCHER of Saltoun two hundred years ago, writing to the Marquis of Montrose and others, said: "I know a very wise man, who believed, that if a man were permitted to make all the ballads, he need not care who should make the laws of a nation." The wisdom of the man and the worth of the saying, have been everywhere recognized. He who should make the ballads of a nation, *would* make its laws of thought, feeling and action; would give the standard by which all laws would be tested,—the condition by which, in the end, they should stand or fall.

And if these ballads had to do with the sacred and universal sentiment of love of country, with heroic deeds and supreme events in the history of a people;—if they embalmed names and scenes which thrilled the heart with every memory—then he who should give them audience with, and charm to all classes of that people, learned or unlearned, old and young, would wield a power to which no formal law could reach.

Considerations like these give a peculiar interest and value to the present volume. Professor Muench, a scholar of extended and varied acquirements, the translator of the poems of William Cullen Bryant into German, fascinated

by the beauty of much of the early and virtually unre-
corded history of South Carolina, gave himself earnestly and
long to the labor of research into the facts and traditions of
our Revolutionary annals, and, as a labor of love, has put
them into smooth, flowing and appreciative verse. They are
more especially designed for the young, and have, most of
them. met the test of arousing an intense and abiding interest
—as others have seen with myself—among our youth. But
they are of scarcely less interest to the older, and even the
oldest. As permanent contributions to the annals of a Com-
monwealth which has been the scene of great events, and the
mother of the great actors in them, but which has lacked the
popular form in which they could become familiar and attrac-
tive to her children, this book should be welcomed and prized
in every home and every school of Carolina. It is the record
of daring and self-sacrifice, with which stately history did not
always nor often deal, save in general statement, but the
details of which quicken the pulse anew with patriotic
fervor.

CONTENTS.

LEGENDS

OF

SOUTH CAROLINA.

LEGENDS OF SOUTH CAROLINA.

The Legend of the Cotton-Plant.

WHEN Father Jove to North and South
    Their various boons had meted,
Their grains and flowers, their cold and drouth,
    And deemed his work completed,
One day in winter-time he met
The Genius of the South, his pet,
Her eye-lid red from crying,
Her voice convulsed with sighing.

"Dear child!" spake Jove, "what troubles thee?
    Why is thy brow so heated?"
"Alas!" said she, "most shamefully
    Thy darling hath been treated!
Two dresses hath the North to show
Of summer's green and winter's snow;
I have but one; determine
That I, too, have an ermine!"

"Tut, tut! dear child!"—spake Father Jove,
    "That thing can soon be altered,
I swear by my paternal love,
    That never waned nor faltered:
Thou, too, shall have thine ermine snow;
So dry, my pet, thy tears and go!"
So cheered and joyous-hearted
The charming Fay departed.

But soon found Jove that he had made
    The host without a reckoning;
That Nature, though he begged and bade
    Was loathe to do his beckoning;
Immutable he found her law;
There was no loophole, was no flaw;
When he assigned his dowers,
He, too, resigned his powers.

Still he must keep for honor's sake
    The word that he had spoken;
His name, his prestige were at stake,
    Had he his promise broken.
He studied up philosophy,
His physics, too, and chemistry,
To find some way or other;
In vain was all his bother.

He then convened his cabinet
  Upon the high Olympus,
And begged his gods, when they had met,
  To shield his glory's nimbus;
He promised e'en a costly prize
To him who would the best advise,
To suit the situation
And his exalted station.

Mars said: "'T is vain to interfere
  In Nature's own dominion!"—
"The thing can not be changed, I fear,"
  Was Mercury's opinion.
Apollo said: "It serves thee right,
To promise things above thy might!"
In short, his Council's action
Gave Jove no satisfaction!

Then Father Jove grew every day
  More gloomy and more somber;
He kept from feast and sport away,
  He found no rest in slumber.
Ambrosia, his favorite food,
He touched no more; e'en nectar could
Delight his taste no longer,
Though Hebe brewed it stronger.

One pleasant day, in early spring
  Pandora came with flowers
That she had long been wont to bring
  To high Olympus' bowers.
She spake: "What ails thee, Father Jove?
Say: art thou ill? art thou in love,
That thou grow'st daily thinner?
Confess, thou cunning sinner!"

Jove told her then how every scheme
  Had failed, though he had striven
To keep his promise and redeem
  The pledge that he had given.
"Well!" laughed Pandora; "I declare!
If that is all thy fear and care,
I rid thee e'en to-morrow
Of thy distress and sorrow!"

With tiny seeds she filled her horn,
  And tying on her pinions,
She traveled forth one pleasant morn
  Throughout the South's dominions.
She dropped the seeds upon the ground,
One here, one there, and all around,
Whence plants sprang forth, that rooted
And grew and bloomed and fruited.

Hence soon, when all the fields were filled
 With bolls of fleecy whiteness,
The Genius of the South was thrilled
 At sight of all that brightness.
"Thanks, Father Jove!" with tenderness
She called, "thanks for mine ermine dress,
Of purest white begotten!"
Such was the birth of—COTTON!

The Legend of the Palmetto Tree.

PALMETTO Tree! Palmetto Tree!
 Fair emblem of the noble free!
Firm as their hands, brave as their hearts,
Thou borest the battle's shattering darts.
Like sharer in their triumph's gain
Thy fame, as theirs, can never wane!

Nigh to the sea, amid a wood
The forest's magnates clustered stood:
Live-oaks and cypresses and pines,
And sycamores enwrapt by vines,
And gazed with looks of proud disdain
At the palmettoes on the plain.

"See that low rabble yonder!" spoke
With haughty mien the lofty oak:
"They pass for trees, but where, I pray,
Bear they a sign that trees display?
They have no branches, bark or cells:
They are tall cabbage-plants, nought else!"

Just then came from the sea-shore's sands
Some men with axes in their hands,
Who called: "Our country to defend
'Gainst hosts and fleets whom tyrants send,
We need stout trunks with iron nerve
And valiant heart. Speak! will you serve?"

"For such an aim we are too good!"
Exclaimed the grandees of the wood.
"As gallant ships that plough the main,
As masts that bear the tempest's strain,
Our towering trunks are fit to use;
To serve as splint-wood we refuse!"

"Take us!" called the palmetto trees,
"And use our trunks just as you please.
E'en though we are but common wood,
'Tis meet and proper that we should
Defend the soil whereon we grew,
That fed us every day anew!"

"A noble speech!" the men replied;
"Nor could we well the task confide
To one more worthy than to you!"
They went to work and cut and drew
The stalwart trees to Sullivan's Isle,
To serve there as a bulwark's pile.

It was not long when o'er the Bay
That bright and smooth in sunshine lay,
A fleet of gallant men-of-war
Was spied approaching from afar,
And making ready to bombard
The Fort that here stood valiant guard.

Shell upon shell, shot upon shot,
Were hurled against the luckless spot;
They dashed the sand like spray around,
They ploughed deep furrows through the ground,
And crashing 'gainst the bulwark, tore
Deep wounds through the palmettoes' core.

Yet stout as rock, with steadfast lock,
They bore the onslaught's every shock;
The hotter waxed the battle's ire,
And fiercer grew the galling fire,
The more their hearts were filled with cheer,
To suffer and to persevere.

Once, only once, they felt distressed
And by the gloomy fear oppressed,
That lost the battle after all,
When, stricken by a well-aimed ball,
They saw their banner from its stand
Hurled at their feet in dust and sand.

Yet quickly was their fear dispelled,
When of a sudden they beheld
A youth leap down, without delay
Pick up the banner, where it lay,
And to its lofty post restore
'Mid cheers that drowned the battle's roar.

And soon there rose another shout
Within the powder-grimed redoubt:
"Hurrah, hurrah! the fight is won!
The foe retreats! our task is done!"
Far o'er the land, far o'er the sea,
Was borne that shout of victory.

But when,—achieved the enemy's rout,—
The brave defenders came without
And saw, how the palmettoes well
Had borne that hail of shot and shell,
Their admiration then gave vent
To this most glorious sentiment:

"They were our comrades, true and brave,
In trials sore, in dangers grave;
Our comrades evermore they be,
An emblem of our victory!
Henceforth the two be linked in fate:
Palmetto Tree! Palmetto State!"

Palmetto Tree! Palmetto Tree!
Fair emblem of the noble free!
Firm as their hands, brave as their hearts,
Thou borest the battle's shattering darts!
Like sharer in their triumph's gain
Thy fame, as theirs, shall never wane!

The Bell of Dorchester.*

BESIDE the Ashley's verdant shore
  Still stands a reverend church of yore,
Alone, alone amid the wood,
Where once a happy hamlet stood.

The time hath been, when round its site
White cottages with windows bright
Caressingly stood in a ring,
As children to their mother cling.

And long ago the time hath flown,
When from its spire the bell-peal's tone
The hamlet's worshippers would call
To prayer and hymn-song at its hall.

And yet though now devoid of bell
The steeple stands, a hollow shell,
Is heard a peal quite plain and clear
Amid the copse at even here.

It seems the spirit of the place,
That time nor changes can efface,
By deepest agony and woe
Impressed upon it long ago.

*See Notes.

It dates from that dread time when fear
Of war had spread its terror here,
When Marion lay before this post
To keep in check the British host;

Then here within the rampart's belt
A true and lovely maiden dwelt,
While her beloved served his land
As ranger under Marion's band.

So close to her who won his heart
And should a foe keep them apart?
Nor prison's doom nor gallows' plight
Could frighten him to miss her sight.

Alas! too oft he tried that risk!
The radiant moon's increasing disk
Betrayed him to the foe at last,
When through the lines again he passed.

He was imprisoned as a spy,
Court-martialed and condemned to die;
In vain the maiden on her knees
Besought the Chief for his release.

In her despair, she then at night
Crept slyly o'er the ramparts' height,
And made her way through bush and swamp,
Unseen by foes, to Marion's camp.

"Sweet lass!" spake Marion, "cease to pine;
I shall be there with all of mine,
To set our mate, thy sweetheart, free!
He shall not die, depend on me!"

The dreadful hour of doom had come,
When to the tune of fife and drum
The youth was led beyond the wall,
Where stood the gallows grim and tall.

And yet no Marion? what detains
The gallant Chieftain and his thanes,
When but five minutes more gone past
The young man will have breathed his last.

The verdict read, the prayer said,
Around his neck the halter laid,
One, one last glance on earth and sky,
The youth resigned him then to die—

When lo! the bell upon that tower
Was rung with wild, impetuous power,
As if it called in utmost grief:
"Come quick! come quick to our relief!"

It was the maid that, crazed with fright,
Had scaled the belfry's dizzy height,
And in her deep despair and woe
Now swung the bell-rope to and fro.

Astonished yet the Britons stood.
When all at once the circling wood
Became alive with shout and shot:
'Twas Marion who had reached the spot.

Then fled the British in dismay
To where their sheltering ramparts lay,
And left the youth, still free from harm,
Beneath the gallows' outstretched arm.

Full hundred years passed since that day
And men have come and gone away;
Still ever since hath at that hour
The bell been tolled by unseen power.

A cynic, sceptic mind in vain
Will try to catch the mystic strain;
A pious, childlike heart alone
Will hear and understand the tone.

— ❦ —

The Magic Word.

A LEGEND FROM AIKEN.

DOWN the dark Unaka Mountain,
  Whence o'er moss-clad, rocky steeps
Bright Tallulah's silver fountain
  Prattling, bubbling, foaming leaps,
The Oconees come descending
  From their vict'ry o'er the Creeks,
Their triumphant voices blending
  With the echoes from the peaks:

"With brave Eagle-Claw for leader,
  Swept our host the enemy's land,
As through groves of fir and cedar
  Sweeps the flame by storm-blasts fanned.
Peace-assured and booty-laden
  To our wigwams back we come;
Meet us, sweet Oconee-maiden,
  With a joyous welcome home!"

And *they* came with footsteps fleeting,
  Singing paeans through the grove;
Every Brave received a greeting
  From his dark-eyed maiden-love;
All save Eagle-Claw, who, taken
  With surprise that he alone
Should so wholly be forsaken,
  Asked in anxious, trembling tone:

"Where abides my Mountain-Flower,
  Hazel-Eye, Oconee's pride?
Why hath she not left her bower,
  Hasting to her lover's side?"
None replied; a painful silence
  Spread o'er all a gloomy pause,
Till the Brave ran forth with violence
  Self to learn their sorrow's cause.

Quick, with eagle's flight he hasted
  To the wigwam on the hill:
On her couch there, pale and wasted,
  Hazel-Eye lay calm and still.
At one glance he saw her ailing;
  'Twas no fever, quick and vague,
'Twas that slow, but steady failing
  Of life's strength: consumption's plague.

Faint her smile now, once so cheery,
  Dull her eye now, once so bright;
Wan her spirit now and weary,
  Brimming once with life and light.
True, a while her lover's entry
  Caused her to forget her pain,
But too soon disease stood sentry
  At her sickbed's side again.

By grave fears and sorrows worried
  That no solace could assuage,
Eagle-Claw arose and hurried
  To the Nation's far-famed Sage.
"Take"—he stammered,—"whatsoever
  Is mine own, make me thy slave;
But redeem by thine endeavor
  Hazel-Eye from death and grave."

Spake the Sage: "Alas! no flower,
  Leaflet, root or mineral-ore
Wields o'er her disease a power,
  That is known to human lore!
Heavenly breath alone can cure it
  In one favored, genial zone:
But admittance, to ensure it,
  Is by 'Magic Word' alone!'

" 'Midst between these rock-girt castles
　　Through whose caves the windblasts sweep,
And the ocean billows, vassals
　　To the storms that rock the deep,
Lies that fairyland-dominion,
　　Lies that earthly paradise,
Fanned alone by zephyr's pinion
　　Wafting through the cloudless skies.

"But a cruel Giant-warden
　　Guards that realm of heavenly breath,
And transgressors on the garden
　　Visits he with instant death,
Save the man, who by discovering
　　One charmed word can stay his sword:
He becomes the garden's sovereign,
　　Yet none ever found this Word!"

"I shall find it; I shall win it!"
　　Eagle-Claw with fervor cried;
Back he went that selfsame minute
　　To his drowsing maiden's side.
"Hazel-Eye! wake, I implore thee!
　　For this very hour we start
For a land that shall restore thee
　　To thy health and joyful heart!"

With a palm leaf-shade held o'er her
　　In his unencumbered right,
On his strong left arm he bore her
　　Onward, southward, day and night:
Buoyed and strengthened in endurance
　　By his love's magnetic spell;
Cheering her by the assurance:
　　"Trust, love! all shall yet be well!"

So they traveled; lighter, clearer
　　Grew the air that blew around,
As each footstep brought them nearer
　　To their journey's utmost bound.
From a hill they last ascended,
　　They surveyed a beauteous scene,
And with joy their way they wended
　　Through a lovely park-demesne.

In an elm-grove, freely oping
　　To the breezes of the West,
On a hill-side, gently sloping
　　To a brook by ferns caressed,
There he built a fairy-bower,　·
　　Spacious, rain-tight, trim and neat,
For his drooping Mountain-Flower
　　For an airy health-retreat.

Scarce had he, this task completed,
  Bedded her on straw of pines,
While he joyed, beside her seated,
  O'er her aspect's hopeful signs,
When the ground, beneath him shaking,
  As from heavy steps far 'way,
Warned him of the undertaking
  That as yet before him lay.

Quick he went to meet the Giant
  Towering like a mountain height,
And by word and mien defiant
  Challenged him to instant fight.
Blow on blow the Giant carried
  With his sword, huge as an oak,
On the luckless wight who parried
  Ne'ertheless his every stroke.

For a while the Giant halted
  In his onslaught on the swain,
And exclaimed, with pride exalted:
  "Well thou fightest, yet in vain!
Tell me then, ere that thou perish;
  Whence the courage thou dost prove?"
Spake the Brave: "What hopes I cherish,
  One and all spring from my—LOVE!"

"Love?" broke forth the Monster, quivering
  In his whole gigantic frame,
While to earth his sword fell shivering;
  "Love? how cam'st thou to that name?"
Paralytic terror shook him
  At this Word of Magic Charm;
Will and strength alike forsook him;
  Nerveless, helpless dropped his arm.

With his weapon's lightning flashes
  Smote the Brave him to the ground;
Then, a torrent from his gashes
  Flowed the Giant's blood around,
Tinting on the plains and valleys
  Crimson-red the yellow clays;
To this hour their color tallies
  With that stain of former days.

Henceforth Eagle-Claw devoted
  To his ward all care and time,
Gladdened, as he daily noted
  How she prospered in this clime,
Till,—restored her health, her laughter,—
  He turned homeward, at his side
His strong maiden who soon after
  Shared his wigwam as his bride.

But when urged to sway dominion
  O'er the lands, from Giant's yoke
Freed through him, his firm opinion
  Nobly thus the hero spoke:
"Not so! void from feuds distressing
  Men elsewhere, this realm shall be:
Heaven's health-giving, bounteous blessing,
  Shall to all be ope and free!"

Long, before the pale face landed
  On these shores, that law was set
And kept sacred, e'en when banded
  Indian tribes in combat met;
Yea! midst all their furious battling
  'Gainst the whites, this holy ground
Never heard their bowstring's rattling
  Nor their war-whoop's angry sound.

On the white race e'en descended,—
  So meseems—that sacred charm;
Whig nor Tory here contended;
  Sherman left it free from harm!
Lovely Aiken! heaven-blest Aiken!
  May thy future well accord
With thy past, in peace unshaken,
  Founded on that "MAGIC WORD!"

———

The Legend of the Rice Plant.*

———

CYNIC speaks with bold derision:
  "Selfish greed and proud ambition
  Move this world!" 'Tis false, that cry!
Faith and Hope and Love are surer,
Infinitely nobler, purer
  Instruments of God on high!

———

Sat a youthful negro-maiden,
Grief-encumbered, sorrow-laden,
  Once on Madagascar's strand:
"He who claims my heart's devotion,
Hath been taken o'er the Ocean
  To an unknown, far-off land.

———
*See Notes.

"Light is every creature's essence;
Light for me dwells in his presence;
　　Darkness reigns, when he is far!
Where he is, I, too, must linger:
Guide my course then with thy finger,
　　Lovers' patron, radiant Star!

"But to cheer his heart with gladness
After days of dreary sadness,
　　What might please him best?—I know!
Most of all he felt enchanted
With the rice that he had planted:
　　This I bring him, when I go!"

Saying so, she rose and hurried
Where her lover's store was buried
　　Underground for winter's use;
Filled with rice a little pocket,
Stored with food her sailboat's locket
　　And departed on her cruise.

Nigh a week she had been sailing,
And her slender stock was failing,
　　Save the rice, that treasured grain;
Yet, though direst hunger pained her,
Still the firm resolve sustained her
　　To preserve it for her swain.

Happily, from far-off Aden,
With Arabia's incense laden,
　　Bound for Barcelona, came
Then the Spanish bark Alascar
Through the Strait of Madagascar,
　　Took on board the famished dame.

So for days, for weeks together
Under fair, propitious weather
　　Sailed the vessel o'er the main,
When abreast the Cape of Blanco,
Like a dismal Ghost of Banquo,
　　Rose a sudden hurricane.

As a deer to lair returning,
Is surprised by hounds, who yearning
　　For her blood, pursue her long,
Till the cruel chase is over
And she finds a shelt'ring cover,
　　Far from the besetting throng,—

So the gallant bark was driven
From her course to westward, even
　　To Columbia's distant strand,

Till—the billows' wrath abated
And the tempest satiated,—
　Safe she reached the welcome land.

Ranged for work upon the trestle,
Ready to unload the vessel,
　Stood a gang of slaves around,—
When a shriek on board resounded
And the dusky maiden bounded
　Down the gang-way to the ground.

Dashing through the crowd, she threw her
At the breast of him who knew her
　Ah! so well beyond the sea:
"He, in whom my heart confided,
See! that Star hath safely guided
　From afar my step to thee!"

Recognition's raptures over,
Gave the dusky maiden-rover
　Her narration plain and short:
How she sailed from Madagascar,
How she met the bark Alascar,
　And in safety reached the Port.

Not an eye of all who listened
Could be seen, but that it glistened
　Moist with tears of sympathy;
Not a hand, that not with pleasure
Gave whate'er it had of treasure
　For the negro's ransom-fee.

With the presents of his donors
Ran the darkey to his owner's
　Mansion-house upon South Bay;
He, on being told the story,
To his honor, to his glory,
　Spurned to take the proffered pay.

"Where the hand of God so plainly
Is attested," spake he. "vainly
　Man defies His high decree!
So, to make me in a measure
Sharer of thy radiant pleasure,
　Keep thy ransom and be free!"

Nestled in a lowly cottage
Was their first repast a pottage
　From the rice, that treasured food.
But the rest they kept and planted
In a little garden, granted
　For their future livelihood.

And it germed and grew and rooted,
And it blossomed and it fruited,
 Founding Carolina's wealth:
Giving work to countless tillers,
Grain to thousand busy millers,
 And to millions food of health!

———

Cynic speaks with bold derision:
"Selfish greed and proud ambition
 Move this world!" 'Tis false, that cry!
Faith and Hope and Love are surer
Infinitely nobler, purer
 Instruments of God on high!

——⊹◈⊱——

Cateechee, the Indian Maiden.*

———

FROM the Broad to Oconee through the Cherokees' lands,
 Rang the blast of the trumpeter-shell,
For these were their Chieftain Kuruga's commands:
"At the tide of the New Moon assemble your bands
 From hamlet and mountain and dell,

And fall on the farms of the cursed pale face,
 Upon Cambridge, their outmost frontier,
And sweep,—with the hurricane's blast through the space
With the rush of the flame mid a forest ablaze—
 Every trace that they ever dwelt here!"

Cateechee, Kuruga's fair daughter, scarce heard
 Of the murd'rous design of her clan,
When deeply her heart in her bosom was stirred;
Yet mustering her courage nor breathing a word
 She resolved upon thwarting their plan.

For dwells not at Cambridge, Frank Allan, her friend,
 Her teacher at school and her guide?
And on him should the tomahawk's vengeance descend?
No, no! 't is her duty his life to defend,
 No matter what fortune betide!

So leaving her wigwam with the daylight's first ray
 And turned to the rise of the sun,
O'er mountain and valley she traveled her way,
Till she reached the Saluda at noon of the day,
 And she followed its southerly run.

———

*See Notes.

Nigh foot-sore she entered a grotto's dim nave
  When the Day-Star stood low in the West,
And she tarried o'er night in the hospitable cave,
And gratefully prizing the shelter it gave
  She named it by "Traveler's Rest."

With the limpid Saluda again for her guide,
  Unwearied the next day she strode,
Till she sighted the village at even's dim tide
And the well-known cot by the rivulet's side,
  Where her teacher, Frank Allan, abode.

"Ah, thou here, Cateechee, so wan and so worn?"
  Spake Allan, amazed at her sight.
"Thy footsoles a-bleeding from bramble and thorn,
Thy tresses dishevelled, thy vestiments torn,—
  Oh, tell me the cause of thy plight!"—

"Full Ninety-Six Miles, as an eagle will soar,
  I traveled to spread the alarm:
Ere stands yet the Moon in the heavens once more,
My brethren's dread war-whoop will ring at thy door:
  Flee quick then to save thee from harm!"—

"Oh thanks for thy warning, thy timely report
  That ransoms from peril our lives!
But to flee from the foe is a coward's resort,
Yet fear not, 't is time yet to build us a fort,
  Ere the host of thy brethren arrives!"

And they builded a fort in the shape of a star
  On the brow of a towering hill,
With bastions that bristled with engines of war,
And ramparts that loomed o'er the landscape afar
  And baffled the enemy's skill.

"But"—questioned the toilers when the work was complete
  And they rested their shovels and picks—
"What name shall be given this shelt'ring retreat?"
"None other,"—spoke Allan—"none other so meet,
  So fit as the name 'NINETY-SIX.' "

"For Ninety-Six Miles, as an eagle will soar,
  This maiden conveyed the report,
That soon will the Indian beleaguer our door,
And seeming it is that the suff'rings she bore
  Shall live in the name of the Fort!"

'T is to marriage that every good story will tend;
  No exception is ours to the rule:
And so, when the Indian blockade was at end,
Cateechee was married to Allan, her friend,
  And whilom her teacher at school.

The Legend of Stony Batter.*

NEWBERRY COUNTY.

WHO ever heard of Stony Batter?
   Few, I dare say: but for that matter,
It shares alike with thousand others
Whose name and fame oblivion smothers;
And so, to wrest it from its fate,
Let me this legend here relate.

A grave-yard, full of wooden crosses,
And ancient oak-trees, hung with mosses,
Was Stony Batter, now discarded,
But once with fear profound regarded
By all the German Palatines
Who dwelt around its border lines.

For ghosts, in long white cloaks attired
And by most savage traits inspired,
'Twas said—were stalking here and roaming
From e'en the early hours of gloaming
Till late at night, so that from fear
None of the neighbors ventured near.

Among these plain and peaceful people
Paul Sutter dwelt, straight as a steeple,
Strong as a bear, bold as a lion,
And like him was his every scion,
Of whom in all he numbered six,
Each fond of boyish pranks and tricks.

It was these youngsters who enacted
The part of spectres, that distracted
The people's minds and set them frantic
By many a masquerade and antic.
'Twas wrong. no doubt; all I can say:
Boys will be boys till judgment day.

One eve in Seventeen Hundred Eighty,
When British yoke pressed hard and weighty,
As everywhere, so on these regions,
And Tories roamed the land in legions,
Paul Sutter's aunt, tears in her eye,
Came to his homestead with the cry:

"Just now a Tory-band of hundred
Came to my house which they have plundered
Of every food, e'en to a platter
I had prepared. of home-made batter!"
Asked Paul: "Where are they?"   She replied:
"They camp close to the grave-yard's side!"

* See Notes

"Here, boys!" spake Paul, "is an occasion
To ply your ghostly avocation!
Don quick your masks, your shrouds, your caskets,
Fill to the brim with stones your baskets,
Bring every tin-pan, plate and pail,
Then follow quickly on my trail!"

All dressed in white, masks on their faces,
Approached the camp with stealthy paces
Across the grave-yard, at whose border
They formed their line in battle-order.
Here, lying low, close to the foe,
They watched his every move below.

'Mid a ravine, enclosed by ledges
And running by the grave-yard's edges,
A fire was seen with figures sitting
Around its hearth, and others flitting
About the camping-grove, till all
Were summoned there by whistle's call.

That was the time by Paul awaited;
For while around their meal belated
They gathered and with mirthful chatter
Discussed that savory dish of batter,
Then with unearthly noises round
A row of ghosts sprang from the ground.

And from their midst a giant towering
'Bove all, called out with tones o'erpowering:
"Now, boys, now give them "Stony Batter!"
And downward came a patter-clatter
Of good-sized stones by well-aimed throw
Upon the Tories' heads below.

"What can this mean?" these asked astounded,
When from their midst a call resounded:
"Why! see you not the grave-yard's spectres
With skulls and shrouds? A thousand Hectors
Avail here not, nor sword nor gun!
Run for your lives! Run, comrades, run!"

Up to their feet the Tories darted
And, leaving everything, departed
With utmost hurry, helter-skelter,
To reach the distant forest's shelter.
On their return next morn they found
Their victuals gone, all else left sound.

But on a ledge, with charcoal written
They read this notice: "Serfs of Britain!
Depart from here and leave this region,
Else dread the spectres' wrathful legion!

The Tories, overcome by fear,
Made haste to leave and disappear.

But when abroad this fight was bruited
And Sutter's feat became reputed,
Then, to perpetuate the matter,
The place was christened "STONY BATTER,"
And to this day it bears that name,
Though few, but few, know whence it came.

The Legend of Altamont, Paris Mountain.

GREENVILLE COUNTY.

" JUST gaze upon this Mountain right
    Of shape and parts organic!
Its narrow crest of even height
    Like as a spine titanic;
Its slopes like ribs of some broad chest,
Its spurs like limbs of one at rest;
And is it not in keeping
With giant huge here sleeping?"—

"I see his trunk, my friend, his spine,
    His chest, his limbs appended,
But where, I ask, is there a sign
    Of skull and neck pretended?
Or was perchance his head one day
Cut from his corse and borne away
By Jack, the Giant-Killer,
To grace his portal's pillar?"—

"No, no, my friend! just step this way
    And view from this direction
The Mountain's shape and thou wilt say:
    That narrow, concave section
Must be his neck—that wooded knoll
His cranium's back part and that whole
BALD ROCK his pate gigantic,
Of barrenness romantic.

"That Giant's name was "ALTAMONT,"
    At Jones' Gap was his station,
Where with his brethren he made front
    Against the Flood's invasion.
So long unbroken stood their chain,
The Flood no entrance here could gain,
To freeze their life-blood's vigor
To soulless, stony rigor.

"But ah! that Giant, bald and old,
 (For thousand years already
Too much upon his strength had told
 And made his gait unsteady)—
He loved the Giantess PINEY MOUNT,
Of winsome form and fair account,
Who lonely and forsaken
Dwelt on the plain near Aiken.

"Long he had wooed the maiden, yet
 In vain was his persistence;
But now, when icy billows threat
 Her welfare, her existence,
He thought by saving her, to prove
His firm devotion and to move
Her heart to feelings tender,
If not to full surrender.

"And so a cloak of emerald green
 He hung upon his shoulders,
(So even now his garb is seen,)
 To hide his rugged bowlders;
A diamond at his front he wore
More brilliant than the Kohinoor,
Which, by the way, I wonder,
None yet secured for plunder.

"And then with strides of seven miles each
 He waded to her quarters,
When yet she stood above the reach
 Of ever rising waters;
Yet dread as was her plight and scare,
When he renewed to her his prayer,
She spurned his pleas with frowning,
Preferring death by drowning.

"Then I shall save thee, spite of thee!"
 He called, and violence breathing
He bore her, ere she yet could flee,
 By force across the seething
And icy waters of the Flood,
With care exploring, where he trod,
Lest slipping he expire
With her amid the mire.

"'T was arduous work to keep the road
 Amid the surging waters,
And at the same time bear as load
 The strongest of Eve's daughters,
Resisting him with all her might,
And tiring him by constant fight,
With struggling, scratching, tearing
The wig that he was wearing.

"At last she slipped into the wave
  From his embrace, and trying
To raise her from her watery grave,
  He fell himself; so lying,
The icy billows of the Flood
Changed each into a lifeless clod
By freezing and congealing
Their blood, their veins, their feeling.

"So, since that day till now, the twain
  Lie side by side extended
Upon the tablet of the plain,
  By charms of verdure blended,
Nought but their outlines well-defined
Revealing to the viewer's mind
Their former nature's essence
And reason of their presence."

—————

The Legend of Paris Mountain.

GREENVILLE COUNTY.

L IKE as a shepherd standing midst his flock,
    Whose watchful eye surveys his grazing sheep;—
Like as a Pharos founded on a rock
    Around whose base the surging billows sweep;—
From earth's deep bowels by volcanic shock
Upheaved of yore,—lords Paris Mountain's steep
Far o'er the plain, a widespread sea of green,
With forest-isles set here and there between.

Upon the Mountain's crest midst copse and fern
    The wand'rer, circumspect and falcon-eyed
For relics of the past, may still discern
    Two lonely grave-mounds lying side by side,
One marked by heaps of stone, as by a cairn,
Its twin by rests of wreaths, decayed and dried.
How came these graves upon this mountain-crest
And who were they that 'neath their covers rest?

A touching legend from the days of old
    Spreads round these mounds a radiant halo's hue,
And meet it is that I should here unfold
    Its deep-pathetic, tragic tale to you
In simple words, just as I heard it told
By one grey sire in memory of two
Who here found peace from trials and from strife,
Man's common boon upon the storms of life.

It was the gallant Keowee-tribe,—they say,—
  That had of yore this neighborhood about
Their hunting-grounds, and wielded here their sway,
  And Paris Mountain served as their redoubt
And signal-tower, from where through smoke by day,
Through fires at night, some watchful, keen-eyed scout
The foe's approach would herald far away
To where the nation's scattered hamlets lay.

Brave Panther-Tooth, chief of the Keowee-clan,
  With breast and visage seamed by many a scar,
The bitt'rest enemy of the pale-faced man
  Whom he had fought in council and in war,—
But now worn out with sickness, weak and wan,
Felt he must die, and hence called Morning-Star,
His brave and only daughter, to his bed,
And, with her hand laid in his grasp, he said:

"I must go hence; my race of life is done,
  Though anxious care would fain detain me here.
Our tribe will choose my predecessor's son
  As chieftain to succeed me, though I fear
He will undo my work when I am gone.
Thou, thou alone, whom he for many a year
Hath wooed in vain, canst counsel him and guide;
E'en though thou loathe him, thou must be his bride!

"Oft have I wished, that, should I hence depart,
  Kind fortune would permit me yet, to lay
Thy hand within the grasp of one, thine heart
  Had chosen as a mate on life's rough way;
So to behold thee at thy journey's start
Would have illumed my end as with the ray
Of glorious sunset that descends upon
A day of dismal storms that veiled the sun.

"But when a nation's fate is threat by strife,
  O'er all our cares then Duty stands ahead.
So vow, thou wilt become the young man's wife,
  (For twice in vain for my consent he plead,)
Wilt guard him, watch him, as thou wouldst thy life,
Wilt warn him, yea! if needs, wilt strike him dead,
Were he to prove a traitor to his land!
Girl! swear it in thy dying father's hand!"

With steadfast voice and with unclouded brow,—
  Tho' throbbed her pulse, tho' ached and bled her heart,—
Brave Morning-Star pronounced the solemn vow.
  "'Tis well, my child! had I not known thou art
My flesh and bone, thine oath had proved it now!
So fling my wigwam's draping folds apart,
That I once more may sit my braves among,
And hear them chant o'er me their funeral-song."

Then by her hand the wigwam's canvas rent,
  Behold! there sat the Indian sachems' train
Ranged in a semi-circle round his tent,
  Intoning one by one the death-chant's strain,
Till in one solemn dirge their voices blent.
With stoic mien the Chief heard their refrain;
Then at his sign raised to a seat of stone,
He spake to them in weak, yet steadfast tone:

"I journey hence, from life's long toil to rest
  Within my grave, and therefore, ere I go,
Receive your dying Chieftain's last request.
  On Paris Mountain, face against the foe,
Have me interred, that e'en my grave protest
'Gainst their advance upon us. Lying so,
Your faith stands pledged to shield my grave till death!"
And with this word went out his life's last breath.

The self-same eve the aged Chief's remains
  Were slowly borne to Paris Mountain's crest
Amid the chant of weird funereal strains
  And there interred, as was his last request,
Face 'gainst the foe. This done, his faithful thanes
For crude memento marked his place of rest
With heaps of stones that scattered lay around,
And then in silence parted from the mound.—

———

Again the Day-Star stood as on the day,
  When Panther-Tooth, the brave old Chief had died.
Again prevailed commotion far away
  Among the Keowees, for at eventide
The time was set, when handsome Mountain-Jay,
Their newly chosen head, should lead his bride
Into his wigwam, where the festive trance
Should be observed with banquet, play and dance.

Hence, soon as tinged the morning's virgin-rays
  The eastern sky with gold, the Indian maids
Had started forth to search the sylvan maze
  For Spring's fair flowers wherewith to tie their braids;
While far and wide the clamors of the chase
Rang through the mountains' inmost haunts and glades,
Where hunters roamed the wilds for bear and deer,
To grace with them the wedding-banquet's cheer.

But sad and pensive meanwhile sat the bride
  Within her wigwam, when its curtained door
By richly-jewelled hand was flung aside,
  And gazing up, she saw her sight before
Her groom, decked out in warrior-chieftain's pride,
The staff in hand that once her father bore,
With panther-skin and wampum round his waist,
And so he spake in tone of eager haste:

"Just now our scout on Paris Mountain's tower
  Brings me a message from my pale-faced friend,
Whereby he bids me come this very hour,
  A council-fire and parley to attend
Where o'er the plain the Mountain's shadows lower.
Though loathe, this day far from my bride to spend,
I must obey stern duty's call and leave:
Yet rest assured, I shall return at eve!"

By ill forebodings thrilled, the maid replied:
  "This day's bright sunlight visits with its glare
My father's grave, as on the day he died.
  Not so his daughter, who might fitly spare,
To deck his mound, some flowers that deck the bride.
So take me there and leave me to that care
Of filial love and dutiful concern,
Till from thy mission's errand thou return!"

With joyfulness he granted her request.
  And so the two went forth through woods and leas
And up to Paris Mountain's lofty crest,
  The bridegroom all the while profuse in pleas
Of fervid love or words of playful jest,
She, stern and mute and cold and ill at ease.
Not till they reached her father's grave, she broke
The seal that locked her lips till then, and spoke:

"I know for what thy friend hath summoned thee:
  To cede this Mount! our nation's all in all,
Their fane, their bulwark and their fortune's key,
  Which once forlorn, they must decline and fall.
I pray thee,"—here she sank upon her knee,—
"I warn thee,"—here she faced him fierce and tall,—
Yield not to them one inch of all these lands!
Depart! thy fate, my fate lies in thine hands!"

Long, long she sat beside her father's tomb
  Upon the lonely mountain's highest crest,
When with the flowers of her own bridal bloom,
  And some she picked, she had his gravestead drest!
The oath that she had sworn, her dismal doom,
And more than these, her nation's future pressed
Upon her heart with greater weight than aye
On this, on this, her festive wedding-day.

The sun had long ago passed o'er her head,
  He stood aslant, sank lower down the sky
And yet *he* came not! What, if he were dead?
  But no! just then espied her falcon-eye
A form come up the hill with tottering tread.
"Alas, 't is he!" so rang the maiden's cry—
"And woe to me! my mind reads in his gait
Both his and mine and our whole nation's fate!"

Long, long she stood in dread suspense, at last
   The drunken Chief arrived before her stand,
His right spread out to clasp the maiden fast,
   A string of glittering beads in his left hand.
"Wretch, knave! stand back!" called Morning Star aghast;
And dashed the glist'ning trinkets on the sand.
"Speak quick: what hath been done? Shall we retain,
Or must we cede our fathers' dear domain?"

"We sold the lands," the staggering Chief replied,
   "We sold them, yet for bounties rich and rare.
Henceforth my love will have her wigwam's side
   With blankets lined and rugs of softest hair.
With ribbons gay her tresses will be tied,
And beads will grace her neck with brightest glare!
Compared to wealth like this, of what account
Is the possession of this useless Mount?"—

"Enough, enough! forbear to wring my heart!"
   The maiden cried in tone of deepest woe;
"Thou canst not bribe me by thy flatt'ry's art,
   Die, traitor, by mine hand!" and speaking so,
Quick like a flash she drew a glittering dart
And plunged its pointed steel with one strong blow
Deep in his breast. He sank with reeling sway
And at her feet a ghastly corpse he lay.

Without delay she left the dismal place
   And set afire a wood-pile near at hand,
For signal-use there 'stablished by her race:
   And when the beacon's flame, by breezes fanned,
And seen afar-off, had with hurried pace
Collected all her friends around her stand,
She spake in broken words from broken heart,
Still holding in her hand the blood-stained dart:

"Friends! Fate ordained, that you should see me wed
   Upon this grave, not at my nuptial room;
It also willed, that in your chieftain's stead
   Whom I have slain, I choose another groom,
Whose name is Death, and that my marriage-bed,
To which I now descend, should be the Tomb!
Receive me then in thine abode of gloom,
A victim of our nation's fatal doom!"

And while her friends still wond'ring stood around,
   She flung her on her father's burial-stead:
But when at last they raised her from the ground
   'Twas but her body and her soul had fled:
Deep in her breast a gaping, ghastly wound
Revealed her deed. With tears and reverent dread
Her friends interred their chieftain's luckless bride,
As meet it was, upon her father's side.

Henceforth these graves on Paris Mountain's height
  The tribe would wreathe with garlands, when the day
Returned amid the years' revolving flight.
  Yea! e'en when forced to cede their lands and sway,
Some of their clan kept up the holy rite,
Till its observance now seems swept away
By Time's, that cruel Vandal's, ruthless knell.
But is this not *our* mem'ry's fate as well?

— ❦ —

The Legend of The White Horse Road.*

GREENVILLE COUNTY.

THEY had their charms, those golden days
    Of stagecoach-travel and relays,
  Of drivers, horses, stables,
Of hostelries and jolly hosts,
Of boards of cheer and merry toasts,
  Of bounteous dinner-tables,—

Of heartier intercourse and ways,
Of kindlier speech than now-a-days,
  Of telling, old-times stories;
And still, all, all went to decay,
And waned and died and passed away
  With their delights and glories,

Since, when the iron horse was born,
Its whistle drowned the driver's horn,
  Its cars replaced the stages,
Its trains left far aside the inns,
Or passed them by with mocking dins,
  Fast as the tempest rages.

Now, such a famous wayside-inn
Was at this century's begin
  Upon a cross-road standing,
Not far from the Saluda-bridge
Upon the summit of a ridge,
  A beauteous view commanding.

A large White Horse as sign it bore
And by that name was known all o'er
  As travelers' genuine Mecca,
By none surpassed in way of cheer,
Since to the kitchen tended here
  The hostess self, Rebecca.

* See Notes.

And while *she* saw to food and fare,
Her husband had the inn in care,
    Of Scotch descent and clever;
From morn till night upon his post,
There never was a better host
    And entertainer,—never!

For boundless funds of tales he had
At his command, both gay and sad,
    And none by fiction tainted,
Yet best he liked, and best he told
Of that White Horse, that, large and bold,
    Upon his sign stood painted.

"Perchance you think,"—he so would say,
"That picture an invention? Nay!
    That horse hath once been living!
Yea more! from danger and from fall
She saved us, suffered for us all,
    Her life as martyr giving.

"It was in Seventeen Seventy Four,
Ten years I counted then, no more,—
    When horse-thieves roamed this region,
Who, two years after, changed their name
For Tories, still remained the same,
    And numbered,—well, a legion!

"Of course, we all were on the watch,
And kept our horses in the patch
    Close by and under tether,
Save one, that horse; she was so tame,
So smart, so wide-awake, so game;
    We left her on the heather.

"Yet she was stolen after all,
For not responding to our call
    One morn in May, we started
To seek her and discovered then
From foot-prints, how a band of men
    Had caught her and departed.

"We grieved o'er her with tenderness,
And fondly hoped we should White Bess
    Yet find and yet recover;
But when the dismal war came on,
We knew she was forever gone
    And every hope was over!

"Then came the time of dreary fright,
When British power was at its height
    And Tories 'neath its banner

From settlement to settlement
Would roam and rob and kill and vent
  Their rage in savage manner.

"One night in Seventeen Seventy Nine,
We were aroused from sleep benign
  By violent stamps and neighing.
We rushed without; there stood the mare,
Bedecked with foam, her nostrils' flare,
  Her bristling hair conveying

"The sign, that peril, nigh and sore,
Impended o'er us, yet before
  We led her to the manger,
She turned and flew to every farm,
There by her neighing to alarm
  The neighbors to their danger.

"And then the river-road along
We heard a band, full hundred strong,
  Approach with furious tearing;
But when the Tories saw our men
Roused by the mare from slumber then
  And for defense preparing,—

"They fired but one shot and wheeled
Back to the forest that concealed
  Their movements by its shelter;—
Then venturing without, we found
White Bessie lying on the ground
  And in her life-blood welter.

"It was the mare for whom they meant
That shot, on her their ire to vent
  For her escape and flying,
To warn her friends, from cot to cot;
And ah! too well was aimed that shot;
  For Bessie, she lay dying.

"Once more she neighed, as if to say:
''Twas not my fault, I stayed away
  From friends I alway cherished;
I struggled hard to set me free!
So kindly, friends, remember me!'
  Then breathed her last and perished.

"And so in gratitude, well due
E'en to a beast, when brave and true,
  I had this Inn denoted
As 'White Horse Inn,' by sign and name,
Her deed of valor to proclaim,
  Her faithfulness devoted."

The Legend of Caesar's Head.*

GREENVILLE COUNTY.

L IKE giant-kings, linked hand in hand,
　And twined by one long verdant band
Of garlands that enwreathe them,
The Mountains of the Blue Ridge stand
As guardians o'er th' enchanted land,
　That east and west lies 'neath them.

Their gorgeous canopy on high
The dome is of the sapphire sky,
　With diamonds spangled over,
While silvery clouds, now far, now nigh,
Like incense-smoke are wafted by
　Or circling round them hover.

Each giant-king's right hand upheaves
A tapering sceptred staff that cleaves
　The baldachin's pavilion,
While Atlas-like his faithful reeves
Upbear the lofty ceiling's eaves
　On testers of vermillion.

Rich gowns these monarchs and their thanes
Wear, clasped by massive rings and chains
　Around their necks and shoulders;
In graceful folds to vales and plains
Their mantles fall, whose gorgeous trains
　Are borne by moss-clad bowlders!

Withdrawn behind Night's sable screen,
Each day they change their wardrobe's mien,
　As seasons may determine;
In spring and summer emerald-green,
In autumn brown with crimson sheen,
　In winter spotless ermine.

Unlike earth's kinglets whose delights
Are petty feuds o'er fancied rights
　For causes small and trivial,
Or childish pageants, pompous sights,
Or festive banquets with their knights,
　Undignified-convivial,—

These monarchs stand in peace profound,
By awe and silence hedged around
　And majesty's true graces;

*See Notes.

Loathe to transgress their kingdom's bound
Or to invade their neighbors' ground,
  They keep their lofty places.

And yet, in case they once should meet,
There stands prepared one common seat,
  Right noble, gorgeous, royal,
With every purtenance replete
To entertain each king and suite
  Of vassals, brave and loyal.

Like fountains, frozen into stone,
Whose jets of spray branch at the cone
  In graceful fans uncounted,
The columns of that Kaiser-throne
Rise plumb into the ether's zone
  By capitals surmounted,

Which, strong Atlantes, bear a Hall,
Cut, chiseled from the living wall,
  Upon their tablets' shoulders,
With antechamber, court and mall,
And crested arm-chairs, broad and tall,
  And desks and copy-holders.

Here, from the beetling verge, the gaze
Sweeps o'er a shelving woodland-maze
  Nigh to the ocean's limit,
Save, when the summer's noonday-haze
Or frowning stormclouds veil the glaze
  Of heaven's clear blue or dim it.

Full many sculptures decorate
This rock-built, rock-hewn Hall of State,
  Surpassing those of Babel;
It boasts a Lion's Mouth and Pate,
A Dragon's Fang, their fitting mate,
  And Satan's Dining-Table.

And yet of all the strangest freak
A Head is, jutting from the peak,
  Of features weirdly plastic,
With nose like as an eagle's beak,
With deep-sunk eye and hollow cheek,
  With mouth drawn deep-sarcastic.

The Sphynx colossal by the Nile,
The Mask on Elephante's Isle,
  Placed by that Face of Nature,
Would but appear as pygmies, while
Its pallor shames the glacier's pile,
  That veils the Jungfrau's stature.

With awe profound the Red Man viewed
That ghastly Face whose eye pursued
  His footsteps wheresoever,
Would on his wigwam's peace intrude,
Would go with him to hunt and feud,
  Would never leave him, never!

From where the wild Chatooga's stream
And Tugaloo the mountains seam,
  To where down in the Lowlands
The Broad and Tyger's waters gleam,
That pale White Face would on him beam,
  As on the Moors frowned Roland's.

And with the progress of the years
Were more and more the Red Man's fears
  Of that Pale Face augmented;
Till from an all-respected Seer's
Wise lips these words rang to their ears
  And were with joy assented:

"A danger grave o'erhangs our race—
We know not what; yet feel its trace
  And fittingly ascribe it
Methinketh, to that Pallid Face;
Hence we must try,—to win its grace,—
  By sacrifice to bribe it!

"So let your Seer appoint, through light
From Manitou, a maiden bright
  Atonement for the Nation,
And let him hurl her from the height
Beside that Face, when day and night
  Join hands in like duration!"

It was a balmy night in June;
On hill and dale the silvery moon
  Shone down from Heaven's high ceiling;
Cascade and brooklet blent in tune;
Fit night for lovers to commune
  In sympathy of feeling.

It was this very spell that drew
That eve two lovers, young and true,
  Away from eyes of spying.
Upon a cliff where stood a yew,
Beneath its dark shade to renew
  Their vows of love undying.

'T was Falcon's-Bill, with record rare
—For one so young—of glory's share
  In battle's trying slaughter,

And Even-Dew, a maiden fair,
Of winsome eyes and raven hair,
  Chief Otter-Tail's sole daughter.

To meet, they oft had sought this hill;
Their tryst to-night though tinged a thrill
  Of deeper sway: of sorrow;
For—a grave mission to fulfill
On far-off journey—Falcon's Bill
  Must leave his maid to-morrow.

Yet when they brought to end their tryst,
They knew not of the angry glist
  From two dark eyes behind them;
And as they parted, nought they wist,
How from the thicket one small fist
  To dread revenge consigned them.

'T was Raven-Eye, the Seer's pet "Bird"
Who had the lovers overheard,
  Their foe and arch pursuer.
By jealousy and hatred stirred
Since Falcon's-Bill she loved, demurred
  To be her swain and wooer.

The third day after, round the Seer
The nation's sachems met to hear
  Great Manitou's decision;
And every father quaked with fear,
Lest he should name his daughter dear
  As victim of remission.

The Seer, while all in silence sate,
Rose and announced the word of fate
  Mid unctuous pleas of duty:
"Hear, men, whom Manitou as bait
To that Pale Face bids consecrate:
  'T is Even-Dew, our Beauty!"

"False priest!" the aged father cried,
"Thy tongue, thy lip, thine heart hath lied
  Beneath the mask of meekness!
So from the wounded eagle's side
The owl will steal his young and hide!
  Up, friends, avenge my weakness!"

Alas! in vain the Chief appealed;
All hearts he found by fear congealed,
  Fear of the Seer's great power,
And so at last was forced to yield;
Poor Even-Dew's dread fate was sealed;
  Her day was set, her hour.

Amid the gloom that dark and chill
Hang o'er her, would her bosom still
　　This hope as comfort cherish:
That yet in season Falcon's Bill
Might come to rescue her from ill:
　　He came not! she must perish!

Around the base of that stark fell
Whence cast that Pallid Face its spell,
　　The Nation was assembled,
When Even Dew bade them farewell,
While wailed the women o'er her knell
　　And e'en the bravest trembled.

In spotless, snow-white samite drest,
Flowers in her hair and at her breast,
　　The lovely maiden wended
Her footsteps up the rugged crest,
By none in this, her crucial test,
　　Save by the Seer, attended.

She stands upon the cliff in sight,
Her face illumed by radiant light;
　　She kneels upon the bowlder;
Again she rises, stands upright,—
The Seer, to fling her from the height,
　　His hand lays on her shoulder,—

Then, then, the folks saw from the rear
A third form on the cliff appear
　　Of manly strength and rigor.
" 'T is Falcon's Bill!"—from ear to ear
The tidings spread.   He takes the Seer
　　And hurls him down with vigor!

With Even Dew, then hand in hand,
He waved good-bye and left the stand
　　And disappeared forever;
Though for their trail the hunters' band
Searched day and night all o'er the land,
　　In vain was their endeavor!—

But when they saw that selfsame year
A band of pale-faced folks appear
　　And forthwith turn their foemen,
It then became to them quite clear,
How had their coming told the sneer
　　Of that Pale Face as omen.

Yet though they bravely fought and long,
And to their utmost, bold and strong,
　　Resisted the aggressions

Of their invaders' waxing throng,
They were at last by might and wrong,
  Deprived of their possessions.

Yet dwells this hope 'mong not a few:
That Falcon's Bill with Even Dew
  Some day will come to see them;
And as from Cæsar's Head he threw
The Seer, so will their foes subdue
  And from their power yet free them!

— ⚘ —

Walhalla.

LOVELIEST of highland-clusters,
  Sweetest forest-loneliness!
Fairy-land of shades and lusters,
  Paradise of wilderness!
Ah! for words thy grace to limn,
Ah! for songs thy charms to hymn!

Blessed is thy power of healing
  Doubting hearts by wisdom's balm!
Soothest every worldly feeling
  By the sameness of thy calm!
Teachest Hope and Faith and Love,
Like a voice from Heaven above!

As my lips drank from thy fountains
  Draughts of Lethe unaware,
As I gathered from thy mountains
  Sweet Nepenthe for my Care,
Let me now, though far from thee,
Solely feel thy witchery.

On me cast thy necromancy,
  O'er me pour thy magic spell;
Fan to life my every fancy,
  Ope my bosom's deepest well,
That, forgetting place and time,
I transport me to thy clime!

All thy charms of beauty blended
  Bring again before my sight;
By thy odors wildwood-scented
  Thrill my heart with new delight;
Breathe thy fragrance, waft thy bloom
Through my city attic-room!

Thou hast heard me; thou hast granted,
  Spirit! my devout requests!
Like a fairy realm enchanted,
  So thy vales, thy mountain-crests
Lie before my raptured eye
Free and open, clear and nigh!

And mine ear culls from the voices
  Of thy breezes tales of yore,
Sweetest science that rejoices,
  Thrills my bosom's inmost core!
These I pen, thy grace to limn,
These I sing, thy charms to hymn!

Lover's Leap.

A Legend from Walhalla.

"MY mind hath read thy heart's desire,
  Mine ear hath heard thy fervid plea,
Mine eye hath seen thy passion's fire,
  And yet I say: It cannot be!
A sacred oath stands in the way,
That bids me answer thee with: Nay!

"The oath I swore that fatal night
  When from the hamlets where we dwelt
The Creeks, our foes, drove us to flight
  And took from me my wampum-belt,
The precious heirloom of our race
And record our descent to trace.

"Without that belt I cannot die!
  Hence if my daughter's hand thou crave,
Restore to me for what I sigh
  And I will bless thee to my grave!
Great is the risk for strength and skill;
Yet the reward is greater still!"

Without a word, without a sign
  The youth went to the open air.
Who stirreth in the wigwam's line?
  His love it is who bides him there.
Around his neck her arms she laid
And spake in accents, meet and sad:

"I know thou goest; I need not ask;
　Yet shall I linger here and pine?
Oh, take me with thee to thy task;
　Then I am thine, thou wilt be mine.
Whatever fate befall us there,
We have therein an equal share!"—

"How can I, Love, refuse thy prayer?
　It makes me twice as bold and strong;
Together we shall better bear
　Both weal and woe; yes! come along!
'Tis seeming that a hero's bride
Be, wheresoe'er he go and bide!"

There was no light amid the grey,
　Yet brighter shone their inward light;
There was no sound upon their way,
　Yet spoke their hearts with stronger might;
So through the silent midnight-grove
Strode on the two in hopeful love:

But when at last they reached the head
　Of one deep chasm, through which a brook
Far, far below o'er pebbly bed
　Ran to the vale, the hero took
The maiden's hand into his own
And spake to her in cheerful tone:

"Stay here, till I return, my Love,
　While stealthily my way I make
Into the enemy's camping-grove
　To get my prize, and meanwhile take
This steel and flint, with them, to light
A fire to lead my steps aright.

"Behold! just now, when I prepare
　To part from thee, there comes a light
From yonder star, whose friendly glare
　First breaks the darkness of the night.
It says: I shall return to thee!
Rely upon its prophesy!"

She was alone! and yet as long
　She heard her lover's footsteps fall,
She felt her courage firm and strong,
　But when e'en these, the last of all,
Had died away, she felt so lone.
As if her peace with them had flown.

Unbroken quite by light or sound
　And like a pall of silent death,

So hung the darkness her around,
  The only sign of life her breath:
Each bosom's throb an agony,
Each moment an eternity!

There came from far,—as if there lay
  Whole worlds between,—a faint report.
Was it some prowling beast of prey?
  Was it a stag's, a beaver's snort?
No huntsman could have made it out,—
The ear of love was not in doubt!

" 'T is he! 't is he!'" she faintly cried,
  Now on the ground, now on her knee:
"Oh Heav'n: be kind to him and guide
  His footstep back again to me!"
Once more her list'ning she renewed,
But soon called out: "He is pursued!"

Quickly she rose   As winds the flame,
  So anxious feelings swayed her heart,
That beat against her bosom's frame,
  As if to break its walls apart.
And nearer, nearer and apace
Rang forth the clamor of the chase.

She heard her lover's far-off call:
  Alas! amid the eager heat
Of headlong flight he missed the wall
  That was for him the safe retreat.
Between his love and him there lay
The yawning gulf now in the way.

With anxious haste the maiden bent
  Her steps along the dread abyss
That ever broader spread its rent:
  One only spot, a precipice,
She knows still where the dizzy steep
Allows the very boldest leap.

She hath attained the wished-for place,
  And while the chase went on across,
With flint and steel she set ablaze
  The brushwood and the withered moss,
So that the glaring flame and sparks
Should serve her swain as guiding marks.

He thus conducted by the light,
  The precious wampum in his grasp,
Now reached the limit of his flight
  And halted there to draw a gasp.
"Leap here, thou hast no other choice!"
Rang from across the maiden's voice.

He leapt! and cleared the wide abyss,
  Since love awaited him across!
One quick embrace, one hasty kiss,—
  They quenched the fire with earth and moss,
And hastened home, but dumb and foiled
The foe stood still and then recoiled.

And comes to-day some loving pair
  As well it may, to LOVER's LEAP,
And hears the legend, sweet and fair,
  They vow as firm and true to keep
Their plighted troth for evermore,
As kept that loving pair of yore.

The Legend of the Grapevine in Walhalla.

IN simple taste, serene and chaste,
  Queen Nature held her year's levee,
When to her throne there came in haste
  Oconee's nymph and mountain-fay.
She cast her at her sovereign's feet
And spoke in accents low and meet:
"Fair Mistress! pray, relieve me,
From plund'rers who aggrieve me!

"For pale-faced men have found my glen
  And marked it for a settlement.
There is no cave, no dell, no den,
  That they not search with base intent.
They even hew my proudest oaks,
My tallest pines by wieldy strokes;
They bridge my brooks, break alleys
Athwart my groves and valleys!"

With peace serene replied the Queen:
  "Calm, child, thy fears! 't is for thy best!
For see! the beauty of thy scene,
  Thy valleys' charms, thy mountains' crest,
Who else but man will judge and praise
And by his works add to thy grace?
What seems to thee distressing,
Thou soon wilt find a blessing!"

Relieved from fear, fleet as a deer,
  Home to Oconee went the Fay.
And though she first found little cheer
  To see her forests cut away,
Yet village-bell and children's song,
White cottages the vales among,
Made her forget her sorrow
And love her little borough.

Still soon again distress and pain
  Brought back the Nymph to Nature's throne:
"Oh Mistress fair! those stalwart men
  Whom I have learned to love and own,
Worn out by toil on stony soil
With work on hills whom sunrays broil,
Have made up their opinions
To leave my fair dominions!"—

"Nay, verily! that must not be!
  The spot, I self most dearly prize,
The place man self most fittingly
  Walhalla named—"The Paradise"—
To lie deserted and forlorn
And of its grace and beauty shorn,—
By my fair name, I vow it,
I never will allow it!"

Thus spake the Queen and to the scene
  She hastened in a moment's space;
Where she found things as they had been
  Described to her at every trace;
The folks disheartened, pale with care,
Worn out by work and scanty fare,
Absorbed in meditation
Of speedy emigration.

"It is quite true: this soil will do
  For neither cotton, rice or grain!
But is there nought, they can pursue?
  If so, my power were quite in vain!"
So spake the Queen and analyzed
The soil and quickly recognized
That none for grapes were better!
"That suits me to a letter!"

A scuppernong the field among,
  That had defied the farmer's axe
And every year had firm and strong
  Come forth and blossomed in his tracks
She now endowed with magic strength,
That, weary of his pains at length,
The farmer deemed it charmed
And let it grow unharmed.

The husbandman, from labor wan,
  Who had till then blamed Nature's stint,
And therefore failed in every plan,
  Now understood her well-meant hint.
"Plant"—he exclaimed—"plant grapevines, friends!
They will most surely make amends
For all our former trials
Our failures, our denials."

So said, so done! and one by one
  The farmer dropped his old pursuits,
Wherefrom he never more had won
  Than meager crops and scanty fruits,
And planted fruitful vines instead
That yielded grapes, both white and red,
And made the place a Vineland,
"South Carolina's Rhineland!"

So prosper then, Walhalla Glen!
  So yield, ye vines, rich fruit each fall!
So thrive, ye worthy vintner-men,
  And with your thrift make this your call:
By healthy vintage, red and white,
To drive Man's fiend, the Rum, to flight
And to efface his notions
For harmful, ardent potions.

HEROINES

OF

SOUTH CAROLINA.

HEROINES OF SOUTH CAROLINA.

The Prize Contest of the Thirteen.*

WHEN not so long ago in social chat
   The sister genii of the Thirteen prime
Colonial founders of the Union sat,
   The consciousness of motherhood sublime
A friendly contest in their midst begat,
   —Such as is apt at any place and time
'Mong loving sisters even to ensue,—
To whom of all the foremost prize were due.

With stately grace the Old Dominion rose
   And so addressed in gentle words her peers:
"Though ladies rarely will their age disclose,
   I boldly boast priority of years.
Here I might rest my case, if so I chose;
   Still let one name me whisper to your ears:
"George Washington" and quickly you will call:
Virginia merits preference over all."—

"Age and renown, frail children of the hour,"
   The Bay-State spoke, "I, too, might claim my own,
And Plymouth Rock and Bunker Hill's high tower
   Proclaim my glory from their speaking stone.
But higher merit I possess and power,
   Learning and art, that make me widely known;
For is my Boston not in prose and verse
Most fitly styled 'Hub of the Universe?' "

Then rose the Keystone State, erect and tall,
   And spake: "My realm extends from lake to sea,
And teems with oil and coal and iron withal;
   And pray, my Dames, what would your Union be
Without your home, my Independence Hall,
   Without its gem, the Bell of Liberty?
And if I name besides my William Penn
And Franklin, ladies, what can you say then?,"

Next came the Empire State and she extolled
   In these proud words the merit of her claim:
' I, too, might pride me of my times of old
   And many are my statesmen I might name.
Yet Age, compared to Life, is drear and cold,
   And Youth surpasses e'en the highest fame!
'T is Life and Youth who made me rich and great
And give me my importance and my weight."

*See Notes.

And so in turn, with more or less applause
  From all the others, every sister plead
With fervid trust and eloquence her cause.
  Fain would I give each speech, but for my dread
Their length would weary you; hence let me pause
  And only briefly sketch the leading thread
Of argument that each Colonial Dame
Announced to prove and demonstrate her claim.

So lauded Maryland her waterways,
  The Granite State her lofty mountains' charms;
Rhode Island gloried in her lovely bays,
  New Jersey eulogized her garden-farms;
While Delaware spoke to her orchards' praise,
  Connecticut extolled her coat-of-arms;
With pride the North State pointed to her mines,
And Georgia to her wealth of yellow pines.

Last rose Palmetto State to make her plea
  And said: "Not on my realm I base my claim,
However wide and fair and rich it be,
  Nor on my statesmen's or my heroes' fame
Though they were great and many as I see
  That more or less you all can plead the same.
A higher prize is mine, a nobler crown:
My daughters' deeds of valor and renown.

'T was they who, when my sons well-nigh despaired
  Would never cease their courage to inspire,—
Who boldly, openly the tyrant dared
  Who mocked his threats and who defied his ire,—
Who sacrificed their all for me nor spared
  For my defense their very roof from fire,—
Who risked for freedom's sake their lives, their health!
The mem'ry of their deeds is all my wealth!"

With one accord the Twelve, most deeply stirred,
  Responded to their sister's fervid plea:
"Far, far, be it from us to doubt thy word,
  Palmetto State. yet would we like to see
Some valid proofs, as we have never heard
  One jot of all thou said'st and we agree:
If what thou claim'st can bear the critic's test,
We will declare thee first of all and best.

No documents on hand, the day nigh spent,
  It was decided that Palmetto State
Would please the vouchers of her claims present,
  When they assembled at some future date.
Hence, soon as she had reached her home, she went
  To see a Scribe and charged him to collate
From books and scrolls and chronicles of yore
The evidence that on her statements bore.

Convinced the work were but an easy sport,
  The Scribe began his task, to him quite new,
But soon was forced to cut his labors short,
  As with his search the proofs in number grew,
Else he would never finish his report.
  This he submits now first of all to you,
If *you* decide these proofs sufficient ground,
Whereon Palmetto State her claim may found!

——⚬——

Marian Gibbes.*

JOHN'S ISLAND lay in peace profound,
  An Eldorado of repose,
When she was wakened at a bound
  By hideous yells and shrieks that rose
On every side and with dismay
So ushered in the break of day.

The reason was: A British host,
  Like countless, greedy locust-swarms,
Had nightly landed on her coast
  And fallen upon her tranquil farms;
Its route of terror marked the horde
By sack and pillage, fire and sword.

Right in the line of their advance
  The pleasant Gibbes Plantation lay;
They halted,—for the stately manse
  A fortress seemed that blocked their way,—
And brought the grim machines of war
To bear upon it from afar.

The mansion's folks were seized with dread;
  Out to the rear through door and gate
In headlong haste the servants fled,
  Regardless of their master's fate,
Who, paralyzed since many a day,
Helpless upon his sickbed lay.

But he was saved through filial love;
  Upon his couch his kinsfolk bore
The suff'rer to a neighboring grove
  Mid leaden hail and cannon-roar.
They set him down on sheltered ground,
Where all his household gathered round.

—— ——
* See Notes.

From here they heard the plund'rers' shout,
  From here they heard the crackling noise
Of flames the Hall within, without,
  When came from anguished lip a voice
That filled with tremor every mind,—
The cry: "The babe is left behind!"

The father called: "My child, my child!
  Will none deliver it from death?"
But all drew back with terror wild
  And spake with 'bated, trembling breath:
"All is in vain! it is too late!
Death were the risker's certain fate!"

Here Marian Gibbes, scarce twelve years old,
  Stepped forth and spake: "Then I will go!"—
"You cannot, child!" but quick and bold,
  She darted through the servants' row
And ran, unheeding prayer and call,
With fleeting step back to the Hall.

Though cannon-balls tore up the ground,
  Though bullets whistled through the air
With more than awe-inspiring sound,
  Above her, round her, everywhere,
She safely cleared the wide expanse
And vanished in the burning manse.

She climbs the stairs with nimble tread,
  'Mid crackling flames and crashing beams.
The babe! is it alive or dead?
  It lives! it lives! she hears its screams;
She gains the room, whence come its cries,
She gains the cradle, where it lies.

Then taking up the child with care
  She closely round it wraps her cloak
And safely bears it down the stair
  Through sparks and flames and blinding smoke.
Though crisped her skin, though singed her hair,
She reached the door and open air.

So soon War's savage minions saw
  What to her deed impelled the lass,
With homage thrilled and wondrous awe,
  They ceased their fire and let her pass.
And so she laid, untouched by harm,
The babe upon its father's arm.

Rebecca Motte.*

NIGH where their limpid waters
   The rapid Congaree
And Wateree commingle
   To form the broad Santee,—
Upon a hill that gently
   Sloped to the river's tide,
Within a beauteous garden
   That hedged its every side,—

There stood a lordly mansion
   Of genuine Southern style,
With vine-embower'd verandas
   And roof of English tile;
Its halls and rooms and stairways
   Replete with gems of art,
And breathing cordial welcome
   That cheers the stranger's heart,—

That asks not 'bout his fortune,
   That cares not for his sect,
But hospitably receives him,
   If but his mien reflect
The gentleman of culture,
   Of honor and of worth;
Nowhere he'd find such welcome
   As on this Southern hearth.

How oft had seen these parlors
   Convene a festive throng!
How oft had rung these hall-ways
   With joyous dance and song!
How often, too, had listened
   Those vine-clad galleries
So cosy, so inviting,
   To Love's endearing pleas!—

What change! the lovely garden
   Cut up by pick and spade!
The trees hewn down and fashioned
   A frowning ambuscade!
The mansion made a fortress,
   With doors and windows barred,
Behind which British soldiers
   With guns held watchful guard.

For rapid like a whirlwind
   And sudden like a ghost,
Had Marion, called the "Swamp Fox,"
   Swept down upon their post;

*See Notes.

Yet though he had beleaguered
  The place since break of day,
Sure of the promised succor
  The foe sustained the fray.

Within the bailiff's cottage,
  Beneath its roof of thatch,
The gallant Chief was busied
  With writing a dispatch,
When hasty steps resounded
  Upon the walk without,
And Lee came in with Davis,
  His faithful Indian scout.

"Lord Rawdon is approaching,
  Not twenty miles away!"
Spake he,—"and will arrive here
  Before the end of day!
To storm the place, our numbers
  Are plainly quite too small;
To stay here will as surely
  Bring danger to us all!

"Yea! were the house a Tory's,
  We lightly could by flame
Compel them to surrender,
  But as the noble Dame
Who owns it, is a patriot,
  'T were wrong to harm her so;
We therefore better hasten
  Elsewhere to strike a blow."

"Then let us go!" spake Marion
  In his laconic way,
And rose to give the order
  To end the fruitless fray,
When through the open side-door
  In stepped Rebecca Motte,
Whom British overbearing
  Had forced to seek this cot.

"All thanks for your forbearance
  Which highly I appraise!"
So spake the noble Lady
  With gentle mien and grace.
"But where to Freedom offer
  So many life and health,
'T is little to surrender
  My house and earthly wealth.

"Behold this bow, these arrows;
  From far-off India sent,
They hung within my parlor
  As idle ornament;
So give them now employment,
  So give them now their aims,
And let them be the agents
  To set my house in flames!"

Spake Lee with youthful ardor,
  His hand raised to the sky:
"Where so in love of country
  Both men and women vie,
What hope for despot's power,
  Though great and dread it be?
What fear for Freedom's lovers,
  To doubt her victory?"

And Marion? Nought he uttered,
  But deep emotion shook
The hero's frame entire;
  The Lady's hand he took,
Up to his lips he raised it,
  While sparkling tears that shone
Within his eyes, made louder
  Than words his feelings known.

Then by a skilful archer
  The sturdy bow was strung:
On sped the fiery arrow,
  Fast to the roof it clung:
Another! still another!
  Its mission each fulfilled,
As if with lust of vengeance
  Their shafts had been instilled.

Soon twinkled in their places
  Three flames as if in sport,
But wafted by the south-wind,
  "The Breeze of Moultrie's Fort,"
They spread their wild contagion,
  And waxing more in space,
They wrapt from porch to attic
  The house in their embrace.

Out rushed in wild confusion
  The British soldiery:
Then blazed from every ambush
  The patriots' musketry:
A bugle-blast! and forward
  They rushed to charge the foe,
When lo! a white flag hoisted
  Announced his overthrow.

Such was the end's beginning,
    First fracture of the chain,
That, link by link, was severed,
    Not to be forged again;
First brought about, remember!
    By woman's sacrifice,
Proud to redeem her country
    E'en at her homestead's price.

— ❧ —

Kate Dillard's Ride.

WHO rideth so swiftly through tempest and night,
    'Mid the peal of the thunder, the flashes of light,
Through the blast of the storm and the downpour of rain,
On a charger, foam-covered on head and on mane?

"'Tis a woman!—A woman? Heav'n watch o'er her flight!
A woman? and out at this season of night?
Can her life be in danger to venture such ride
'Midst perils whose terrors the bravest had tried?

Still nobler a motive, still higher an aim
Have counselled her action, our wonder to claim:
To rescue her brethren from ruin and fall:
That, that is her errand at the risk of her all,

At the risk of her welfare, at the risk of her health,
At the risk of her fortune, her homestead, her wealth!
And well she hath reckoned the cost of her flight;
For gazing behind, what confronteth her sight?

The firmament reddened in the direction she came
By a dread conflagration, by fire and flame!
"'Tis our cottage!" she mutters,—"well, let it burn!
The safety of hundreds is greater concern!

"To reach them, to warn them, before 't is too late,
I escaped from the foes, while at supper they sate,
And rode to the southward, to foil their pursuit,
But returned to the highway by a roundabout route.

"But hark to that clatter! They are Ferguson's men!
Down, down in the vale on their ride to the Glen.
By the time that you reach there, ye lords of the torch,
Mine host, to receive you, shall stand at the porch!"

And onward she galloped for many a mile,
Till stopped by a challenge from wooded defile:
"Who comes here?"—"A woman, a Whig and a friend,
With tidings whose purports all scruples forfend!"

Her message scarce heard, not an instance was lost,
And dummies, full many, were dressed and disposed,
Like soldiers asleep and of lifelike display,
While the men hid in ambush till the break of the day.

And then in the bushes a rustling was heard,
As if by the breezes the foliage were stirred;
Then followed a whisper, and then a command,
And forth on the dummies rushed Ferguson's band.

"Surrender!" they shouted, but not a reply;
"Surrender!" then thundered the patriots' cry,
Prolonged and re-echoed by voices of men,
Who, weaponed for battle, arose from the Glen.

And so the surprisers themselves were surprised,
To rout and defeat them, few minutes sufficed;
Full hundred were captured, full hundred were slain,
Full hundred were scattered through forest and plain.

And all through the battle, like another Joan Arc,
Kate Dillard was leading with Colonel Frank Clarke;
But, an Angel of Mercy, when the fight was at end,
She attended the wounded of foe and of friend!

Betty Moore.

WHERE the wild Savannah's fountains
    Rend in twain Chatooga's mountains,
        At the door
To the lower valley's garden,
Like a grim and silent warden,
        Stood Fort Moore.

As a colt foams 'gainst his bridle,
As a lion 'gainst bars,—so idle
        And in vain
Were the Red Man's pains to rid him
Of that valiant Fort that bid him
        Shun the plain.

Long ago these foes, impeded
By that stronghold, had receded
        Farther West;

Wherefore still those cannon frowning
From its walls, those bayonets crowning
          Its tall crest ?

Ah! by Power, through Fortune risen,
Freedom's Tower was made her prison
          And her grave,
O'er whose mound now that dread giant,
Tyranny, let his defiant
          Banner wave.

Where free men, self-armed and willing,
Without discipline or drilling,
          Years ago
Had, for hearth and home inspired,
Gathered, guarded, fought and fired
          On the foe,—

Hirelings now, well-trained and banded,
By stern officers commanded,
          Here held sway,
Paid to do their master's pleasure
And enslave the land by pressure
          And dismay.

Through the fear spread by this legion
Freedom's cause was in that region
          Nigh stamped out:
Butler's band of patriots only
Still maintained it, weak and lonely,
          Yet devout.

"Let us quench to-night these embers!"
Major Innis bade the members
          Of his staff;
"Lead your every man to Grand View,
Where their band hath had its rendez-vous
          Long enough.

This through boys, who served as drummers,
Learned a lass of sixteen summers,
          Brave and sly,
Betty Moore, who with her mother
And with Ben, her younger brother,
          Dwelt near by.

"I must warn my friends, must see them,
From their foes' arch plot to free them!"
          Musing so
For a while, she called: "I have it!
No, not I! 'T is God who gave it
          How to go!"

Guarded, as she knew the high-way,
By patrols watched every by-way
    And by spies,
Her sole route remained the river,
How she might her friends deliver
    From surprise,—

Yea! the river leading straightway
From the mountains' narrow gate-way
    And defiles
To the patriots' well-known rendez-vous,
Nearer than the road to Grand View
    By twelve miles.

Like expert with boat and paddle
As with rifle and with saddle,
    Oft by day
She alone had undertaken
Rowing down the stream, unshaken
    By dismay.

But at night a mate she needed
To direct her, as she speeded
    Her canoe
Safe past shoals and rocks that lour
'Neath the waters to devour
    Boat and crew.

"Ben might help me, were he present!"
Ah! just then, in hand a pheasant
    He had shot,
Came her brother who consented
To the scheme she had invented,
    On the spot!

In his left a pine-knot lighted
To illume their path benighted,
    So sat Ben
Crouching at the bow and spying
For the snags and ledges, crying
    Now and then:

"To the right! —The left!— Row slower!
Eddies here! The channel lower!"
    While abaft
Betty sat and by her paddling
Deftly steered the quivering, waddling
    Little craft.

So they shot past frowning ledges,
Cliffs with sharp and jagged edges
    Through the night,

Aided in their undertaking
By the friendly moon's awaking
      Silver-light.

Smoother grew the current,—nigher
Grand-View's hills approached—and higher
      Rose their joy.
To be near their destination,
When with sudden agitation
      Called the boy:

"Right! Quick to the right! dear sister!"
Ah! too late! A snag sinister,
      Half afloat,
Stove a hole through prow and siding
Of the frail and swiftly gliding
      Luckless boat.

Happily two trailing willows,
Bending o'er the surging billows,
      Stretched their hands
To the ship-wrecked crew and drew them,
As by life-lines, nearer to them
      On the sands.

'Reft now of the pine-knot's blazes
Through the tangled jungle's mazes
      Crept the two,
Creeks and tree-trunks intervening,
Thickets sky and landscape screening
      From their view.

Torn with wounds from thorn and briar,
Worn with toil through copse and mire,
      Chilled with damp,
On they strode, this thought their cheerer:
Every step will bring us nearer
      To the Camp!

Now a wooded hill ascending,
Through its grove their footsteps wending
      By the light
Of the moon, what vision causes
All at once that Betty pauses,
      Thrilled with fright?

'Mid an oak-tree's leafy bower
She discerned a panther cower,
      Crouch and creep,
On them fixed his eyes of fire,
Stealing slowly nigh and nigher
      For a leap.

Quick to shove Ben 'hind a boulder,—
Snatch the musket from his shoulder,—
    Turn it round,—
Was an instant's work. So standing,
She awaits the monster's landing
    To the ground.

And he leapt! Like lightning's flashing
Quick she turned, the musket crashing
    On his head,—
Saw him wheeling, saw him glaring,
For another leap preparing,
    Fierce and dread,—

When two shots nearby resounded
And the beast fell deadly wounded;
    Not too soon!
For a moment more she eyed him,
Then exhausted fell beside him
    In a swoon!

Soon restored to life and feeling,
She beheld Ben by her kneeling
    In distress,
While upon his side two strangers
Stood with muskets,—patriot-rangers
    By their dress.

Sent from camp upon the mission,
Its bare larder to provision
    For a feast,—
Searching round for game at night-time,
It was they who in the right time
    Slew the beast.

Now relieved from fears and dangers,
Safely guided by the rangers
    On their way,
Soon the two came to the camp-ground,
Where the patriots on the damp ground
    Sleeping lay.

"Yet in time! Thank God!" So voicing
Her full heart's devout rejoicing,
    Betty's call
Rang aloud: "Men, wake from slumber!
Foes approach, ten times your number!
    Rouse ye all!"

To their feet the patriots bounded,
Grasped their weapons and surrounded
    Betty Moore,—

Saw amazed this apparition
Like an angel stand their vision
  Here before,

Read amazed the plain assurance
Of her perils, her endurance
  In her sight,—
Heard with spell-bound admiration
And surprise the brief narration
  Of her flight!

Was it strange then, while they listened,
That their eyes were dimmed and glistened
  Moist with tears,
That they proved their grateful pleasure
By their hands' affectionate pressure
  By their cheers?

"Friends!" spake now their Chief with fervor,
"Shall but tears thank our preserver?
  Shall she go
Home where ills must overtake her?
Our last breath stands pledged to make her
  Safe from woe!

"Now, no better we can free her
Of her fear, than safely see her
  To her door;
While the foe pays *us* a visit,
Let *us*—'t is too good to miss it—
  Take Fort Moore!

"By no other deed beseeming
We can hope the debt redeeming
  To this maid:
Not till o'er Fort Moore your banner
Waves in proud, victorious manner,
  It is paid!"

Joyfully his men assented
To the venture he presented;
  Leaving four
To receive their guests expected,
All the rest their march directed
  To Fort Moore.

Thence at midnight, never dreaming
That their foes had learned their scheming,
  Innis' men
One and all set out, proceeding
Swiftly down the highway, leading
  To the Glen.

Smould'ring still they found the embers
Of the fires, but all the members
     Of the band
Had departed. "We must find them,"
Shouted Innis, "Keep behind them
     Close at hand!"

Lured by shouts and shots and blazes
Southward through the forest's mazes,
     They pressed on,
Eager to entrap their foemen,
Yet where'er they came, the yeomen
     Long had gone.

Meanwhile o'er a secret by-way,
Shorter than the rambling highway,
     Butler's corps
Hastened and past guard and sentry,
Led by Betty, held their entry
     In Fort Moore.

Thither, worn by fruitless roaming,
Innis' men returned at gloaming,
     But to find
On them closed their gate-ways, on them
Aimed their guns and those who won them
     Ranged behind.

Long hath vanished every vestige
Of the Fort, its walls, the prestige
     That they bore:
Betty Moore's bright fame and glory
Will endure in song and story
     Evermore.

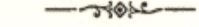

Martha Bratton.

"LONG live the King! Rebellion lies
  Bruised, crushed, stamped-out for ever,
And nevermore shall Treason rise
  To lift with rash endeavor
Its insolent, unhallowed sword
Against our King and Sovereign Lord!"

This was what Cornwallis wrote
  In victor's haughty fashion,
When a courier brought him a note,
  That set him wild with passion.

"What!" smould'ring still Rebellion's fire,
When I had deemed it quenched entire?"

What caused his anger, was to read
  How rebels, few in number,
Had under Colonel Bratton's lead
  Surprised his men at slumber,
And,—what enraged him most of all—
Well-nigh within his sight and call.

"Up, Captain Huck, collect your men!"
  The irate Chieftain thundered;
"And fall upon the traitors' den
  At best a paltry hundred,
And bring me, to receive his due,
Each member of that rebel crew!"

They rode and when they reached the spot,
  Broke through the door of batten;
Then rushing wildly through the cot,
  Inquired of Martha Bratton:
"Where is the Colonel?" Then said she:
"With Sumter, where he ought to be!"

A Scotchman, wroth o'er this reply,
  Then seized with grim intention
A reaping-hook that hung close by,
  When by the intervention
Of Captain Huck the lady's life
Was spared from the assassin's knife.

They searched the house from ground to top,
  From cellar to the gable;
They rummaged every barn and shop,
  They went through yard and stable;
No Colonel Bratton anywhere,
And still they knew he had been there.

"Our bird hath flown! To horse ye all!
  We may yet overtake him
At Williamson's Plantation Hall
  And from his sleep awake him!"
They reached the place, but found him not,
And worn from ride, camped at the spot.

But faster, o'er another way
  Had Martha's servant ridden,
His mistress' message to convey
  Where Sumter's men lay hidden;
He, never slow to strike a blow,
Forthwith fell on the slumb'ring foe!

They rose, but to be stricken low,
  They fought, but vain their labor;
Too strong the patriots' every blow
  They found from gun and sabre.
When rose the sun that morn in June,
He shone on fields with corpses strewn.

But few escaped by speedy flight,
  'Mong them a wounded Tory,
Who galloping with all his might,
  Exhausted, pale and gory,
Reached Martha Bratton's cottage-door,
Where faint he sank upon the floor.

'T was he who eve before had threat
  Her life in wanton fashion,
But now his doom so quickly met,
  Like him void of compassion;
For judged, he was condemned to be
Suspended from the gallow-tree!

But Martha spake: "Give him to me!
  'Gainst me he hath been sinning!
To me he came with mercy's plea,
  My heart's compassion winning,
And mercy should to him be given,
As mercy 't is I hope from heaven!"

The action of a noble mind
  Will spread, its bounds transgressing;
So Martha's deed was not confined
  To him who felt its blessing,
But, circulated far and wide,
Won hundreds o'er to Freedom's side.

Dicey Langston.

HOME from school, with footsteps lighter
  Than the breeze that plays its way
'Mong the leaves,—with glances brighter
  Than the smiles of summer-day,—
So a winsome maiden wanders
  Now through grove and now through lea,
Where 'mid oozy banks meanders
  Twinkling, sparkling Enoree.

Reaching now her home, she fleeted
  To the chair, where she had left
On that morn her father seated,
  Of his sight through age bereft;
Heretofore their daily meeting
  Ever breathed delight and cheer,
But to-day the old man's greeting
  Spake of nought but pain and fear.

"Father! why these traits of sorrow?"
  Spake the maiden woe-begone.
"Left thee hale and bright this morrow;
  Is it aught that I have done?"
Thereupon with accents tender
  Spake the father, while he pressed
With his arm the sweet and slender
  Maiden to his loving breast:

"Ah, my child! I cannot scold thee,
  I should self thy way pursue,
Were I strong, as oft I told thee.
  Right to love and right to do.
Still we are forlorn and lonely,
  One bound in the other's fate,
And our wicked foes know only
  Ah! too well our feeble state!

"For this morning, storming, blundering,
  Came a crowd of Tories here,
And in tones of violent thundering
  Made me swear through threats and fear
To enjoin thee, that thou never
  Wilt again their plans betray,
Or henceforth by thine endeavor
  Aid the Whigs in any way!"

"Ha! these valiant knights, these heroes,"
  Spake the maid with passionate ire;
"Ha! these tiger-hearts, these Neros,
  To assail a helpless sire!
One regret now thrills me solely,
  That I was not born a man,
So to wreak my vengeance holy
  On these ruffians' heartless clan!

"Still for thy sake I will pledge me
  To their plans to close mine eye,
Since concerns for thee now hedge me
  Like as barriers, strong and high,—
Save when I shall find them scheming
  'Gainst my brother's life and weal:
This shall be a cause beseeming
  For my irksome vow's repeal!"—

Spake her father: "None can blame thee
  For thy brother's sake to part
From thy pledge, that lets me claim thee
  As still dearer to mine heart!
Well I know, how hard thou find'st it
  Thine heart's eye to shut to wrong,
Yet for mine own sake thou bind'st it
  With a bandage tight and strong."

Time wore on; from hour to hour
  Bolder grew the Tory-clans,
By the British, then in power,
  Helped and favored in their plans.
Dicey kept her vow unbroken,
  And though knowing oft their aim,
Nor by sign nor message spoken
  Gave away their treach'rous game.

But one day she saw them making
  Ready all their guns and men
For some greater undertaking
  Than they had essayed till then.
Never thinking, never dreaming
  What could be their base intent,
She discovered, that their scheming
  Meant the Elder Settlement.

In this thriving, little village,
  Thirteen miles by country-road
From her place, engaged in tillage,
  Dicey's brother, Will, abode.
Should these Tories, armed for battle,
  Fall upon him, when in bed,
Rob him of his goods, his cattle,
  Burn his cot and strike him dead?

Hasting home then and imparting
  To her sire the ruffians' plot
And her firm resolve of thwarting
  Their designs upon the spot,—
Spake her father: "Go, my daughter!
  From thy pledge thy lips are freed;
Right thou dost to foil their slaughter!
  May kind Heav'n thy footsteps speed!"

To the river-bridge she hasted,
  But aware 't was guarded then,
Dashed, without a minute wasted,
  'Long the bank through swamp and fen,
Till, attained a spot, evading
  Watchful eyes, she crossed the tide,
And by swimming, paddling, wading,
  Safely reached the other side.

Gliding through defiles and thickets,
  Shunning every human soul,
Watching well for Tory pickets,
  Late at eve she reached her goal.
All she found in slumber buried
  At the village, on the farms,
But they quickly woke and hurried
  To defend their homes by arms.

Soon the Tories came, but seeing
  Every house warned of their raid,
They retreated, homeward fleeing
  With the cry: "We are betrayed!"
Vowing vengeance 'gainst the traitor,
  Centred their research on one,
Dicey Langston, who far later
  Had returned, her mission done.

Dicey, well their plot divining,
  Kept at home, till once enticed
To a friend by art designing,
  This short moment's space sufficed
For the Tory-gang to gather,
  Hurry to the cot and break
Through the door, on Dicey's father
  Bloody, dire revenge to take!

Then, just then, as if pervaded
  By presentiment of ill,
Dicey saw, by sharp sight aided,
  Groups of men upon the hill
Near her cottage surging, striding,—
  Instantly surmised their plot,
Leaped upon her horse and riding
  Furiously just reached the spot,—

When her sire, to say his prayers,
  Five short minutes was allowed,
And surrounded by his slayers
  Knelt before the heartless crowd.
Breaking through them, sideways flinging
  Those who held him in their grasp,
Called the maiden, to him clinging
  With a strong and loving clasp:

"Murd'rers! must you vent your ire,
  Vent it on the guilty head,—
Me, who bear the blame entire,
  Kill me in my father's stead!"
Softened by her filial daring,
  Dropped the Tories rope and knife,
And forsook the cottage. sparing
  To her prayers her father's life.

Love Will Abide.*

IN Newberry County, the traveler may note
   'Twixt the Broad and the Saluda the trace of a moat;
'T is known as the Dead Line the neighborhood o'er,
A line that divided the settlers of yore;
Since northward the Scotch and the Irish abode.
While the Germans prevailed to the south of the road,
Each party intent upon guarding its side,
Forgetting the precept that: Love will abide!

One morn through the Dutch Forks was spread the alarm
From homestead to homestead, through village and farm,
That Gretchen, Dutch Gretchen, the settlement's pride,
Was stolen at night-time by Billy McBride.
Detected too soon in their furtive design,
The two were o'ertaken when crossing the line;
Reproved for her venture, Dutch Gretchen replied:
"You cannot divide us, for: Love will abide!"

Now so it would hap, that at the same hour
Dutch Hans had abducted Scotch Bess from her bower,
The sweetest, the fairest dear blossom of all
That bloomed at the manor of Duncan McCall;
Their flight was discovered and, hotly beset,
Was stopped at the Dead Line, when—who should be met?
But the captors of Gretchen and Billy McBride.
"Cheer up, Hans!" spake Bessie, "for: Love will abide!"

And so the two parties, the culprits between,
Stood facing each other with threatening mien;
Each father demanding his daughter's return,
Each lover objecting with ardent concern,
Each maiden, as tranquil, as if 't were not her case,
Till, at last, after various discussion of ways,
'T was left with the damsels, the point to decide;
What else was their verdict but: "Love will abide!"

For Gretchen responded with obstinate will
By a pout of her rose-lips: "I cling to my Bill!"
And Bessie retorted with a sidelong glance
Upon her beloved: "I stand by my Hans!"
Then blending their voices, they spake in duet:
"Friends! neighbors! why will you so sternly be set
On mutual suspicion, refusing as guide
The truest of sayings, that: Love will abide!"

*See Notes.

There were two bright weddings, as well you may guess,
When Bill wed his Gretchen and Hans wed his Bess,
But a wedding far greater, than either of these,
Was the union of neighbors in concord of peace,
Resolved the Dead Line from their hearts to efface
And mingle in friendship as one and the same race,
To cherish their country and ever confide
In the truth of the precept that: Love will abide !

— ⤙◈⤚ —

Jane Thomas.

WITHIN a dark and gloomy cell
      Of Ninety Six, the Citadel
   Of British Reign of Terror,
In durance vile two patriots lie
To pine and writhe, perhaps to die,
   For Freedom's love, their error.

But worse than prison, worse than death,
Their fate is: through infected breath
   Within that dark enclosure
The smallpox-scourge hath smit the pair,
Here twice as dread through lack of care,
   Through hardship and exposure.

'T is Colonel Thomas and his son,
Those gallant Spartan chiefs that won
   Bright fame at Moultrie's Island;
'T was this that brought on them the doom
To lie within the prison's gloom,
   Dragged hither from their highland.

And yet, amid their deep despair,
God gave to them a blessing rare,
   The wife's, the mother's presence,—
Jane Thomas', who by love and skill
Dispelled the shades of sickness, till
   They gained their convalescence.

That she her nursing could pursue,
Was not to British mercy due
   Whereof it seemed to savor:
Her labor's precious sacrifice
Within the fortress, was the price
   Wherewith she bought that favor.

So, free to pass through fort and line,
One eve she learned the foe's design
   To start on instant mission

To Culbertson's, the Patriot's, Inn
Who, as they knew, kept in his bin
   Stored Sumter's ammunition.

Quick to her husband's side she ran
And told him of the enemy's plan;
   Then spoke the noble Spartan:
"We must,—we must defeat their ends,
And save these stores, whose loss our friends
   Would grievously dishearten.

"Fain I would risk it, were I not
Held chained by sickness to my cot;
   Such, too, is John's condition!
On thee, dear wife, the true, the brave,
Devolves this task our stores to save:
   Thou must perform the mission."—

"But," spake she,—"will they not on you
Wreak vengeance, when they gain a clue
   Wherefore I have absconded?"—
"That lies with God! 'T is ours to do
Our duty whatsoe'er ensue!"
   The gallant chief responded.

Jane Thomas, soon as waned the day,
Slipped from the Fort and made her way
   To Brown's, a patriot yeoman:
From him she loaned a horse and sped
O'er by-ways till she came ahead
   The slowly marching foeman.

Unseen by eye, she gained the house
And quickly went to work to rouse
   Her friends from midnight slumber.
She found the convoy's men had gone;
So Culbertson, his wife, his son
   And she, but four in number,—

Were to defend the precious stores;
Yet, brave and bold, they barred the doors
   And set their guns in order;
Prepared for stout defense they stood,
When came the British from the wood,
   That girt the homestead's border.

Then, while the father down below,
The son upstairs fired at the foe,
   Now here, now elsewhere standing,
The women whom no fright could stun,
Were busy loading gun on gun,
   And to the marksmen handing.

In vain, the foe poured shot on shot
Against the log-built, strong-walled cot,
    In vain the doors they battered;
They were repulsed with nigh a score
Of comrades slain and many more
    With limbs by bullets shattered.

Then knowing safe her friends' abode,
Jane Thomas, quickly mounting, rode
    Back o'er the self-same by-way;
She reached the Fort at break of morn,
Ere yet the foe, fatigued, forlorn,
    Came marching back the highway.

So fast had been her ride, so sly,
That, hard as would the Britons try,
    They never could discover
Who 't was that gave their plan away,
Till leaked the secret out one day,
    When long the war was over.

— ⚜ —

Rachel and Grace Martin.

"TELL us a story, Grandpa, do!
    A story, funny, long and true!
And ten sweet kisses, two from each,
Shall be the payment for thy speech!"
Such bribes I hardly can resist;
So, children, sit quite still and list:

It was in Seventeen Eighty One
When at a farm near Lexington,
A British Ensign, gaily drest,
Had for a night put up as guest;
His hostesses (no men were there)
The Misses Martin, young and fair.

The Ensign, when the meal was o'er,
Disclosed quite frankly that he bore
With him dispatches from his Chief,
That promised prompt and strong relief
To Major Cruger and his men
At Ninety-Six, beleaguered then.

"But fear you not,"—the ladies said—
"To be attacked, to be waylaid?"

What? he afraid? nor host, nor ghost
Could frighten him—so ran his boast,
Till came the time good-bye to say,
As he must start at break of day.

Next morn, quite early, ere a soul
Was yet astir, two figures stole
Out of the Hall, in male attire,
Their faces hid by masks of wire,
With shaggy beards, with hats of felt,
With knives and pistols in the belt.

They ran to where amid a wood
Two grooms with horses waiting stood;
Beside their steeds one held a horn
And one a drum.   At break of morn
All quickly mounting, dashed away,
While yet in sleep the Ensign lay.

He, too, rose early to pursue
His journey with his retinue
Of two dragoons and rode for hours,
When, all at once from leafy bowers
Two uncouth men sprang in his way
And seized his rein and bade him stay.

"Hand o'er the papers that you have,
Or else find here an unknown grave!"
They thundered and with this request
They aimed their pistols at his breast,
While from the woods just then the clang
Of drum and bugle loudly rang.

The two dragoons, moved by the fear,
That many hundred men were near,
Turned round and fled with speedy gait
And left the Ensign to his fate.
What could he do?   It was quite plain:
Resistance here would prove in vain!

Forced to submit he handed o'er
The sealed instructions that he bore;
With these one groom was from the scene
Forthwith despatched to General Greene.
Of highest import.—let me say—
The papers proved in every way.

'T was noon, when to the manse again
Returned in haste those figures twain;
'T was eve, when tired, disconsolate,
The Ensign reached the mansion's gate.
His hostesses from eve before
Received him kindly at their door.

"What? back so soon from Ninety-Six?"
"Alas!" said he, "a host of Whigs
Drove my dragoons to hasty flight,
And what was I 'gainst such a might?"—
"He erred! there were *two* hosts, not one!"
The ladies said, when he had gone!

"Now, children! say: can you surmise,
Who were those figures in disguise?"—
"Ha, ha! we knew that from the start:
The two young ladies played that part!"—
"How know you that, my pets? Proclaim!"—
"Because we should have done the same!"

———⟶⟨⟩⟵———

Emily Geiger's Ride.*

PROLOGUE.

"LISTEN, my children!" so at a time
    A poet immortal began his rhyme,
And a world entire, with footsteps fleet
Gath'ring around him, sat at his feet,
Like nursery-children, so still and intent,
With eyes wide-open in wonderment
And folded hands, all anxious to hear:
"The Midnight Ride of Paul Revere!"

Thrice happy New England! whose annals inspire
To hymnals undying her minstrel's lyre,
Where ev'ry brave deed and valorous act
—As the brightest of metals the lightning attract,—
Is certain its herald and poet to find,
To be written and read with devoted mind,
To be valued and cherished and held as dear,
As "The Midnight Ride of Paul Revere!"

'T were well, if all others would follow her lead;
'T were well, if each gallant and chivalric deed,
Where'er it occurred in the days of yore,
Were hallowed for ever through minstrelsy's lore.
And so, that the matter at once may be tried,
I'll tell of another historical ride,
A hardly less valiant and glorious career
Than "The Midnight Ride of Paul Revere!"

*See Notes.

Emily Geiger.

At an early hour of a dawn in June,—
Still stood in the heavens the disk of the moon,—
A crowd was assembled in front of a cot
In a motley, half-anxious, half-curious knot
Round a jet-black charger, all-saddled for ride,
And they fondled his neck and they patted his side,
Affectionately murm'ring: "Remember, good steed!
This day a whole country depends on thy speed!"

The intelligent creature in mute reply
Let sweep o'er the circle his faithful eye,
And eager to prove to the people his strength,
Extended his forelegs their uttermost length,
And seemed to express by his snuffing the air,
By the strain of his muscles and nostrils' flare:
"Be tranquil, good folks! I shall prove by my deed,
That the country not vainly relied on my speed!"

The cottage-door opened and out on the scene
And led by the arm of General Greene,
Came Emily Geiger, her thoughtful face
Illumed by her mission's transfiguring rays.
But he gave her a letter, and stroking her curls,
He whispered: "God shield thee, thou bravest of girls."
Then turned to the charger: "Remember, good steed;
This day a whole country depends on thy speed!"

A kiss from her father, who lent her his aid
To leap in the saddle,—a word from the maid,—
And forth plunged the charger with all his might
And quickly had vanished with falcon's flight.
Long hearked yet the patriots to his gallop's report,
Then turned to their task of bombarding the Fort;
But they prayed the whole day: "Oh haste thee, good steed!
This day a whole country depends on thy speed!"

In a course as straight, as a robin will soar
To the North, when the winter's dominion is o'er,
The maid in the mean time had followed the ridge
That skirts the Saluda: once over the bridge,
Her journey lay wholly in hostile domain,
A region of warfare and party-campaign;
So she called to her charger: "Now haste thee, good steed!
The weal of a country depends on thy speed!"

A ride of five hours—and the Enoree lay,
From mountain-rains swollen, across their way;
Every bridge washed away, every trace of a ford;
No ferry, no wherry to take them on board.
Yet breasting the billows, they boldly defied
The treacherous, turbulent, threatening tide,
And landed in safety! "Now haste thee, my steed!
The weal of a country depends on thy speed!"

'Twas noon! and from heaven the radiant sun
Shot fiery beams, yet she slacked not her run,
As she wended her way through the Tyger's vale
On a narrow, obstructed, old Indian trail.
Her saddle here broke, but she flung it aside,
And sitting now bareback, continued her ride,
While urging her charger: "Now haste thee, my steed!
The weal of a country depends on thy speed!"

So riding, two Tories, their muskets in hand,
Sprang forth from their ambush and brought her to stand!
They asked her; unwilling her word to believe,
They ransacked her satchel, but failed to perceive
How she swallowed the letter she bore at her heart;
The search proving fruitless, they let her depart.
Remounted she whispered: "Now haste thee, my steed!
The weal of a country depends on thy speed!"

'Twas eve! in the tent-rows of Sumter's small camp
Sat his men round the fires, when a furious tramp
Was heard of a sudden, and a charger flew past
With the roar of a whirlwind and the pant of a blast;
His rider a maiden with wild-flowing hair,
But her visage illumed by a rapturous glare,
As she called: "Yet one moment, one moment, my steed,
And saved is the country, yea! saved by thy speed!"

Inquiring for Sumter, wherever she went,
Scarce waiting for answer, she came to his tent
And spake: "It is Greene who hath sent me; his note
I swallowed when waylaid, yet know what he wrote.
To give him a chance yet, the Fort to assail,
Or else to retreat when his efforts should fail,
He bids thee 'gainst Rawdon forthwith to proceed;
For the weal of the country depends on thy speed!"

And Sumter believed her; he gave the command
Forthwith to assemble his mountaineer-band;
And while the drums rattled and the clarions blew,
The maiden went out to her charger and threw
Her arms round his neck, while exclaiming with joy:
"Friend! Knowest what meaning these signals convoy?
The thanks of a country for thy valorous deed:
For saved is the country, yea! saved by thy speed!"

EPILOGUE.

My task is completed; my story is told,
As I found it inscribed in the annals of old;
And heard it recounted by gray-haired sires
On winter-eves by the chimney-fires.
With you it remains now to judge and decide:
If Emily Geiger's heroical ride
Deserve not to rank as a worthy compeer
Of the "Midnight Ride of Paul Revere!"

Kate Fowler.*

FROM Ninety-Six, the British Fort,
  Comes o'er the plain the grim report
    Of fierce and angry battle
Where cannon roar with deaf'ning sound,
And mortars swell the din profound
    And musket-volleys rattle.

It seems, as if the Fort were doomed:
Its ramparts that so proudly loomed
    To heav'n, are rent asunder,
While nearer, ever nearer creep
The enemy's works and batt'ries sweep
    Its walls with louder thunder.

There on the ramparts Britain's Chief,
Brave Cruger, spying for relief,
    Stood in the midnight-hour:
"Haste, Rawdon, haste! Unless thou come
By noon to-day, we must succumb
    To Greene's superior power!"

At self-same hour, the other side
Had called a Council to decide
    Like grave a situation:
Lord Rawdon, by their scout's report,
Was coming to relieve the Fort
    And to attack their station.

Beside the two main parties yet
Another was by care beset,
    By anxious heart-throbs proven,—
A maiden who had overheard
Within a closet every word
    And plan that had been woven.

Kate Fowler 't was who—plain and short—
Loved Major Cruger of the Fort
    With true and warm devotion,
And hearing now the wily foe
Design her lover's overthrow,
    Conceived the daring notion

To run to him across the line
And tell him of their arch design
    To force him to surrender!
But—if she fell, ere reaching him?
Well! first a letter she would limn
    To warn the brave defender.

————
* See Notes

So, sitting down, in haste she penned
A billet to her lover-friend,
  Whose like was never written,
Of Rawdon's coming, Greene's intent,
And love and farewells strangely blent,
  Were she by bullet smitten.

————

That morn, a nimble-footed youth
—(But tell me, was it one in truth?)
  Went forth with firm decision,
A well-sealed letter at his breast,
And leaping o'er the bulwark's crest
  Departed on his mission.

"See that deserter! see that spy!"
Rang forth the loud and angry cry,
  Then muskets blazed and thundered;
Yet onward ran the youth unharmed,
As if his very life were charmed,
  That all who saw it, wondered.

Already he had gained the breach!
One leap! had brought him out of reach
  Of guns and under cover;
When ah! just then the fatal ball,
Too surely aimed, brought him to fall;
  His race of life was over!

Then from his breast, so that they knew
He bore grave news, the note he drew
  And held it 'loft, while lying;
So, men without a minute's loss
Sprang from the ramparts to the fosse
  And brought him inside dying.

Within the Fort the bearers met
Their Chief awaiting them and set
  The stretcher's bed before him;
To him the youth the letter gave,
And motioned him by feeble wave
  Of hand to bend down o'er him.

Scarce had brave Cruger bowed his ear
Close to the youth upon the bier,
  Called he with wild emotion:
"Kate, thou? my Kate! it cannot be!
So much, so much thou didst for me?
  Great is thy love's devotion!"

He held her still in his embrace
And with his tears he bathed her face,
  While lit a deep contentment

Her traits, when oped the enemy's side
Their firing, and the Fort replied
  With thunders of resentment.

Then by his plan, 'gain and again
Greene stormed the Fort with might and main;
  He could not take the barrier;
Chief Cruger put his schemes at nought,
Well-posted through the letter, brought
  By Kate, his martyr·carrier.

But when the grim assault was o'er
And Greene retired for ever more,
  By Rawdon's coming frightened,—
Chief Cruger ran without delay
To where his love, his heroine, lay
  Who at his entry·brightened.

"Thank God! thou livest still, my dear."
He called, "the glorious news to hear,
  Our triumph's cannon fired!
To thee alone we owe, to thee!
Our rescue and our victory!"
  Then smiling she expired!

— ❧ —

The Heroines of Castle Pinckney.*

AUGUST 21, 1888.

"IN the morningbeam's ray lie the Harbor and Bay;
  No fairer a promise gave ever a day
To a fisherman's fondest of wishing!
To the sea, to the brine, brave companions of mine!
Let us hasten this morning with tackle and line
  For a royal enjoyment of fishing!"

To so tempting a call, seven comrades in all,
With quickness responding, made ready their yawl,
  For the jacket their city-dress doffing.
With the tide at its best, with the breeze from the West,
Like a sea-gull their galley skimmed over the crest
  Of the waves to the banks in the offing.

There a shoal by the Fort, at the gate of the Port,
To the fishermen known as the fav'rite resort
  Of sheepshead, they chose for their station:
Then the canvas made fast to the pole of the mast,
Neath the surface below them the anchor they cast,
  And proceeded to ply their vocation.

*See Notes.

And they gathered a store, such as never before
From the depth of the waters their baited hooks bore,
   Yet with minds to their harvest attending,
Failed their eyes to remark how the sky had grown dark,
And a hurricane's phantom from heaven's high arc
   Upon them was swiftly descending.

With a tiger's fierce leap, with a falcon's bold sweep,
It fell on the drowsing, the unaware deep,
   Overturning the bed of the ocean:
With the lightning's bright flash, with the thunder's loud crash,
It broke on the stillness and whipped with its lash
   The brine into instant commotion!

As, a prairie afire, one only desire
For a refuge the animate world will inspire,
   So the waves here for shelter were hastening
Through the channel's close gap to the harbor's safe lap;
Yet worse was their fate here, for caught in a trap,
   They suffered the hurricane's chastening.

Ere th' unfortunate crew of the fishing-boat knew,
From the anchor their galley was sundered and flew
   Where the tempest and billows would lash her;
Neither rudder nor oar would prevail any more,
Resistless the waters must drive her ashore,
   Where the breakers to pieces would dash her.

From the harbor-wall's height had a watcher caught sight
Of the fishermen's struggles, their perilous plight,
   And quickly his call had collected
The busy, the idle, the people withal,
Who gathered on pier-head, on house-top and wall,
   Their eyes on the galley directed.

Ere a move could be made to come to their aid,
When precious each moment of rescue delayed,
   Ere a tugboat was ready or steamer
To their rescue to hie,—through the crowd rang the cry:
"The boat is upset! they must perish and die!"
   And they watched them with anguish and tremor.

Then out from the rear of the Castle-wharf's pier
Saw the people a shadow,—a row-boat—appear,
   Two rowers were seated within it!
Now lost to the eye, now perched upon high,
Unwearied they labored until they came nigh
   And nigher the drowning each minute.

With a breathless suspense stood the multitude dense
On their progress intent, when a billow immense
   Cast them backward and sideward some distance;

Yet, their balance regained, every muscle they strained,
Till by efforts redoubled their goal was attained
  In the teeth of the tempest's resistance.

O'er the gunwale the two with celerity drew
One by one of the shipwrecked and perishing crew;
  To the land then directing their vessel,
Without ceasing they rowed, till they landed their load
In the sheltered retreat of their island-abode,
  And they set them ashore on the trestle.

Then arose from the piers a succession of cheers:
"Hurrah! the two heroes, undaunted by fears
  Of the perils from tempest and water!"
Till aloud from a spar rang the voice of a tar:
"What say you: two heroes? Two women they are!
  'Tis the Warden's brave wife and his daughter."

"Not the first time it is, that the briny abyss
Through their courage and prowess its victims must miss,
  Though they reaped no reward and no glory;
But henceforward a crown of the brightest renown
Will encircle their names and forever hand down
  Their remembrance through song and through story!"

HEROES

OF

SOUTH CAROLINA.

HEROES OF SOUTH CAROLINA.

Fort Johnson, 1765.

JUST as the man whose excellent merit
 Glaring achievements of others conceal,
Resteth content, that the world will inherit
 Richly the fruits of his labor and zeal,—

What! if humanity fail to applaud him,
 Holding his service at trifling regard?
Little he recks the attempt to defraud him;
 In his own bosom he finds his reward!—

Such is the spirit that hovers and breathes
 Over and 'round thee, historical spot!
Laurels that mem'ry round other points wreathes
 Ought to have fallen by right to thy lot!

Long before men as Indians attired
 Gutted at Boston that cargo of tea,—
Long ere the shot that at Concord was fired,
 Thundered its echoes o'er land and o'er sea,—

Here at Fort Johnson, proud Albion's tower,
 Lording o'er Charles Town, its harbor and bay,—
Here at a time when Tyranny's power
 Undisputed still wielded its sway,

Here, even here, was set the example
 Calmly, yet nobly, how freemen should meet
Despots and hirelings who venture to trample
 Justice and liberty under their feet!

Hear then the story! It was in November
 Seventeen Hundred and Sixty and Five,
—Year of the Stamp Act, as well you remember,—
 When a fleet sloop here was seen to arrive.

Overtly chartered, the Fort to provision,
 Stamps were her cargo; the people on shore
Quickly suspected her secret commission,
 Vowing to heaven: "Not a stamp shall come o'er!"

Not with the clamor of public bravado,
 Not with the mumm'ry of wig and of mask,
Not with the blast of a furious tornado,—
 Earnest and silent they went to their task.

Hundred select men, most ably commanded,
  Met about midnight with musket and oar,
Traversed the river in row-boats and landed
  Long before morn on the opposite shore!

Ere from their slumber the man that stood sentry,
  Wakened his comrades through gunshot's report,
Quickly the hundred had rushed through the entry,
  Forced to surrender the guard of the Fort.

Quite a strange spectacle, novel of manner,
  Greeted the skipper at dawn of the light:
High on the ramparts an azure-blue banner,
  Underneath gunners prepared for the fight.

Brief was the parley that raised the embargo,
  Laid on the vessel by cannon's stern mouth;
Back to Great Britain she sailed with her cargo,
  Never a stamp was sold in the South.

Mute as they came, so the hundred departed,
  Duty's fulfillment their only reward!
Knowing the tyrant for evermore thwarted,
  Little they cared for historian or bard!

Well done, Green Mountain Boys at Ticond'roga!
  Yet from Fort Johnson you copied your feat!
Boast of thy victory, proud Saratoga,
  Yet with Fort Johnson thou canst not compete!

Here was a bond 'twixt the thought and the real,
  Here a due balance of actions and needs;
Here was presented man's highest ideal:
  Noblest of sentiments, noblest of deeds!

Isaac Hayne.

Dulce est pro patria mori!

IN dreary winter-season
  Consigned to prison's bane,
Condemned to death for treason,
  Lay Patriot Isaac Hayne;
Yet calmly to his fate resigned,
He to his end thus spoke his mind:
*"If on the field or gallows high,
'Tis sweet for Freedom's sake to die!"*

With tears their father's pardon
  His little girls implored
From Britain's chief Crown-warden;
  Yet was their prayer ignored.
Allowed one last, sad interview,
Their father thus bade them adieu:
*"If on the field or gallows high,
'T is sweet for Freedom's sake to die!"*

For mercy Charles Town's ladies
    Blent in one fervid plea;
Yet stood as firm as Hades
    The Judge by his decree!
When told, that vain their efforts proved,
Spake Hayne with cheerfulness unmoved:
*"If on the field or gallows high,
'T is sweet for Freedom's sake to die!"*

Then framed a strong petition
  Brave burghers of Charles Town,
But to receive derision
  And meet with scorn and frown.
No more their failure could dismay
Hayne's strength of spirit than to say:
*"If on the field or gallows high,
'T is sweet for Freedom's sake to die!"*

'T was Hayne's last day. Admitted
  Through prison's gloomy gate,
His son, by grief unwitted,
  Bewailed his father's fate.
"Weep not, my son!" was Hayne's request;
"Thy comfort be my last behest:
*"If on the field or gallows high,
'T is sweet for Freedom's sake to die!"*

The hour had come! Arisen
  From sleep, Hayne bade adieu
To all his friends in prison,
  Who weeping round him drew.
Said Hayne: "Pray, comrades, cease your grief,
And joy with me in this belief:
*"If on the field or gallows high,
'T is sweet for Freedom's sake to die!"*

The jailer's "Are you ready?"
  He answered with: "I am!"
And marched erect and steady,
  Devoid of boast or sham.
His step so firm, his gait so free,
Voiced his conviction's steadfast plea:
*"If on the field or gallows high,
'T is sweet for Freedom's sake to die!"*

He stands beneath the gallows,
  Upon the judgment scene;
A heavenly radiance hallows
  His face with peace serene.
They draw the black cap o'er his eye;
Then rings his last triumphant cry:
  "If on the field or gallows high,
  'T is sweet for Freedom's sake to die!"

— ❦ —

Kosciusco.

SOUTH CAROLINA! speak, art thou aware,
  What hero's footstep hallowed once thy shore,
And what illustrious, sacrificial share,
  For thine own good he gladly, freely bore?
What wrought his mind for Freedom's guardian care,
  A pillared shaft tell at the Hudson's door;
How by his arm he vouchsafed Freedom's prize,
No stone, no song, no legend testifies.

It should not be! The living memory,
  The rightful boast, the undisputed claim,
That a Kosciusco fought and bled for thee,
  Should blazen forth as brightest diadem
From all thy glories' matchless galaxy.
  The hero-martyr's image, at whose name
Two continents in deep-felt homage bow,
Should wreathed with evergreens adorn thy brow!

Arise, historians, and with reverence trace
  His spirit's likeness on the fervent page!
Here, poets, find a theme of epic grace,
  As will your highest fancy's flight engage!
Here, sculptors, is your type to carve a face
  Of three in one, the hero, martyr, sage!
While I content me, from his brief abode
Within these parts, to tell this episode:

A welcome lull, like as a grateful calm
  Upon a storm, had spread o'er the domain
Of bloody war,—a cooling, soothing balm
  On burning wounds inflamed by fever's pain;
A foretaste of that peace, whose fragrant palm
  All hearts so oft, so long invoked in vain,
When lo! once more War's frightful tocsin broke
The quietude with sudden thunder's stroke!

Beneath the fav'ring screen of darkest night,
　　And of their foemen's countersign possessed,
A British force had landed out of sight
　　Upon the Ashley's tree-girt shore, and pressed
With a tornado's fierce and sudden might
　　Upon the patriots, who, surprised, distressed,
Gave way before the onslaught's violent storm,
Till rallied by Kosciusco's towering form.

Then all at once rose o'er the battle's din,
　　O'er bugle-call and musketry and shout,
A woman's shriek of anguish from within
　　A cabin set ablaze amid the rout;
A bed-rid cripple, left by all her kin,
　　When, terror-fraught, War's tumult rose about,
She must become a victim to the flame,
Unless the boldest, quickest rescue came.

But who should save her life, as midst between
　　The hostile lines the wretched dwelling lay?
Or who would risk his own for one so mean,
　　So worthless quite in every human way?
And yet these men, inured to every scene
　　Of savage warfare and of bloody fray,
Stood shuddering there and felt their blood congealed,
As that poor woman's screams rang o'er the field.

No sooner struck her shrieks Kosciusco's ear,
　　When, instantly resigning his command
To his Lieutenant standing in his rear,
　　And in the scabbard thrust his faithful brand,
He started on his mission, void of fear,
　　To save the victim's life by his own hand.
Unharmed by balls, he reached the burning cot
And bore the cripple to a sheltered spot.

Then as by charm the British fire was hushed,
　　And from their lines that stood with arms at rest,
A white flag in his hand, their leader rushed
　　Up to Kosciusco, whom he thus addressed:
"Tell me thy name, brave man!" The hero blushed
　　And modestly complied with the request.
Surprised, spell-bound, to hear the name renowned,'
The Briton stood, then spake with awe profound:

" 'T is all we can, our banner to defend
　　'Gainst gallant men whom freedom's aims inspire;
Yet if their cause such men as thou befriend,
　　Whose word and sword fan their devotion's fire,
'T is useless, hopeless, further to contend,
　　And no disgrace when vanquished we retire.
This now we do, cheered by the thought serene
Of mankind's triumph in this War's last scene!"

Marion's Leap.*

"DRINK, Marion, and accept my toast:
　　We shall defy the British host
　　　As we defied their galleys!"
So rang the challenge, wild and bold,
Across the banquet-hall of old,
　　In one of Charles Town's alleys.—

"We shall defy the British host,
Though not by loud, vain-glorious boast,
　　But warfare long and steady,
Demanding all our strength and cheer;
So let me now depart from here,
　　To set my weapons ready!"

"Thou shalt not leave! Bolt fast the door!"
Rang through the hall the deafening roar;
　　Then leaped the gallant Ranger
By one impetuous, sudden bound
Out of the window to the ground,
　　Regardless of the danger.

He fell upon the pavement-stone,
And striking broke his ankle-bone;
　　Though aid was quickly tendered,
Long on his couch the hero lay
At his plantation far away,
　　While Charles Town was surrendered.

That was a providential leap,
Fraught with results so grave and deep
　　As never leap attended!
Though followed in its wake by pain,
It proved his and his country's gain,
　　A trial with blessings blended.

The leap that Marion risked that day,
From senseless bout to break away,
　　For Freedom's cause reserved him!
Blind, blind the eye that cannot see,
That this was done by God's decree,
　　That God Himself had nerved him!

_____
* See Notes.

1780.

A S with the terror of the tomb,
  As with the silence of the grave,
A shroud of woe, a pall of gloom
O'erhang the land, whose youthful bloom
  So fair, so bright assurance gave.

As is Cocytus' hollow groan
  The only sound in Hades' shades,
So echoes now the land alone,
With measured tread and martial tone,
  From ocean-boards to mountain-glades.

Hushed is the faintest sign and sound
  Of hearty mirth, of cheerful glee;
For fear of spies that lurk around,
Men speak in whispers, on the ground
  Their glances fixed, once frank and free.

Hath every arm been stricken lame?
  Hath every hand grown numb and weak?
Hath every bosom bowed to shame?
Hath every tongue forsworn the name
  Of Right and Liberty to speak?

So, so it seems, but only seems;
  For while purblind, vainglorious Power
Complete and sure his triumph deems,
And vict'ry's fruits already dreams
  Within his grasp,—that very hour

Adversity, a nation's test,
  As it is man's, hath nerved and steeled
With one strong impulse every breast,
To rise, to struggle, not to rest,
  Till Tyranny's defeat is sealed!

So, calmly bearing wrong and shame,
  They bide the leader "frank and bold."
Whose clarion shall the hour proclaim,
When all shall rise in Freedom's name,
  For vict'ry and revenge enrolled.

It rings! as if fair Freedom's hand
  Self set the trumpet to her mouth
And sent abroad her blast's command,
So strong. so bold, all o'er the land
  Peals Marion's summons from the South.

As o'er the prairie sweeps a fire,
  So swiftly spread the bold alarm,
From town to town, from shire to shire,
Till stood ablaze the land entire
  From lowland-swamp to mountain-farm.

Undrilled, scarce-armed, these men defied
  The flower of British soldiery;
And ere the year had wholly died,
King's Mountain's Battle turned the tide,
  And swept their host back to the sea!

Song of Marion's Rangers.[*]

WHO are they that yonder so daringly ride
    Through forest and clearing and heather?
No river too rapid, they plunge through its tide,
No thicket too tangled, they brush it aside,
    They reck not the darkness, the weather!
You hear not a signal nor word of command:
It is Marion's gallant, invincible band!

But yesterday roaming along the Pedee,
  They fell on the camp of the Tories,
Who, weening the Rangers far by the Santee,
Were busied with feasting in frolic and glee;
  Then rudely disturbing their glories,
The champions replied to the sentry's demand:
"We are Marion's gallant, invincible band!"

A hundred miles west by the Cooper to-day
  They lie mid the bushes in hiding;
A train of the British is coming that way,
Well guarded by escorts; yet without delay
  The Rangers are 'mongst them by riding.
The flying are captured and sabred who stand:
All by Marion's gallant, invincible band!

At Georgetown the foeman sought refuge by flight,
  By ramparts defended from danger,
When all of a sudden with hurricane's might
A squadron of horsemen emerged into sight
  And vaulted the ditches, each ranger
Proclaiming this warcry, while waving his brand:
"We are Marion's gallant, invincible band!"

* See Notes.

Who are the gay rev'lers whose voices arouse
  The owls in the groves of Snow Island?
The tent of a live-oak for shelter and house,
On booty they conquered, the rangers carouse
  With the mirth of a chase in the Highland;
And then in a chorus their voices expand:
"*We are Marion's gallant, invincible band!*"

They care not for glory, they care not for gain,
  They serve not for pay or for ration;
For Freedom they battle, from Tyranny's chain
To deliver their land and from servitude's bane
  To ransom forever the Nation.
No power on earth can such valor withstand,
As thrilled Marion's gallant, invincible band!

—⁂—

Scipio's Feat.

'TIS neither the Elder nor the Younger I mean,
  Whose fame Madam Clio has writ on her screen,
That sets forth the mem'ry of the greatest and best,
But veils with oblivion the names of the rest,—

But Scipio, a negro, the servant and slave
Of Marion, the Swamp Fox, the gallant and brave;
He followed his master wherever he went,
As cook and as hostler in camp and in tent.

Once while at Snow Island they lay in the swamp,
A scout brought the message, the welcome, to camp,
Of a train with provisions, with clothing and shoes,
On the road to Fort Watson, for the garrison's use.

"They hardly require them, we need them far more!
Up, comrades, to gather the harvest's rich store!"
They saddled, they mounted, they galloped,—too late!
The train was already in the fortress' safe gate!

One, one only hogshead lay forlorn in the road,
Rolled down from its wagon, o'erweighed by the load;
To seize it the Rangers dashed forward.—in vain!
They moved not the hogshead, but their wounded and slain!

For lying in sight of the fortress and nigh,
Its marksmen could lightly all ventures defy,
By force or by cunning, to carry away
The hogshead in question, the coveted prey.

So Marion stopped further exposure of lives;
"For," said he, "what grief for your sweethearts or wives,
If not for a Tory's or Englishman's head
But a *hog*shead their loved ones were hurt or shot dead ?"

Then Scipio stepped forward to Marion and spake:
"Permit me, dear Massa, one venture to make!
I give you my promise, I shall be alert,
Not to get me in danger to be caught or be hurt!"

"There is ham, there is bacon! I smell them afar!
No booty so precious we met in this war!"—
"No, Scipio," said Marion, "you stay in your nook!
For useless are victuals in default of a cook!"

Reluctantly Scipio his master obeyed,
And hid 'mong the bushes, from where he surveyed
That hogshead with pensive and covetous mood,
Till shortly again before his master he stood:

"Oh Massa! allow me, I beg you, one look!
For what without victuals is the use of a cook? "
Then struck by the force of the reason's intent
With laughter the master gave the slave his consent.

Stretched out at full length in the swamp-grass, the rake
Crept forward and onward with the stealth of a snake,
Till he gained a stout pine-tree by a hazardous bound,
While harmlessly whistled the bullets around.

There, there lay the hogshead,—so near, yet so far,—
Upon it directed all engines of war;
Yet Scipio proved equal to the height of his task,
And quickly determined, he fashioned a mask.

On a sapling he fastened his jacket and hat
Not sparing his idol, his crimson cravat;
Then planting the dummy in the ground to the right,
That it drew for a moment the garrison's sight,—

To the left side he bounded with the leap of a hind,
And ere yet had vanished the smoke in the wind,
The negro lay snug in the hogshead's safe port,
Unbeknown to the British on the walls of the Fort!

"The hogshead is rolling! is moving down hill!"
Called then from the ramparts some voices, "and still
Not a speck, not a sign of a motor is seen!
Look well for the hider, when he leaveth his screen!"

Just then came the crisis, for a sudden descent
Gave the cask a momentum, no strength could relent;
To his feet then the negro rebounded and ran,
While the hogshead with thunder close followed his van.

On the ramparts the marksmen attempted to shoot;
They could not for laughter, to see the pursuit
Of the man by the hogshead which, on reaching the line,
Was stopped in its progress by the trunk of a pine.

And Scipio's olfactory presage proved true:
There was ham, there was bacon, quite savory and new;
For a right royal dinner he fried them in part,
While the praise of the Rangers delighted his heart.

Andrew Jackson.*

WITH every mark of need and want,
    Unkempt, barefooted, ragged, gaunt,
Yet proving by his every trait,
That he was born for better fate,—
A boy, scarce fourteen years of age,
Came riding, perched behind the stage,
To Camden, where he asked the host
To trust him with an hostler's post.

"On Waxhaw's fields our cottage stood,
A peaceful home amid the wood,"
—The boy explained—"when Tories came
And drove us out by sword and flame.
On Waxhaw's fields my father died,
As rebel was my brother tried,
My mother sank from wan despair,
And lies interred, I know not where!"

And while he spake, no tear or sob
Revealed his bosom's inmost throb;
Yet every muscle in his face,
His every eye-glance bore the trace
Of iron will and steadfast nerve,
As will not from their purpose swerve;
And so impressed, gave him mine host
With quick assent the asked-for post.

And well the youngster, from the start,
Performed his duties' every part;
The stalls had never so been swept,
So well the colts and horses kept,
As since the day, when Andrew here
Began as hostler his career,
And had he time, unasked he would
Work round the house, at what he could.

* See Notes.

But since the British troops had come
Into the Town with fife and drum,
And since the officers of grade
Their quarters at the Inn had made,
He kept the stable day and night,
As if he loathed their very sight,
Nor would he deign a word or look
On British servants, groom or cook!

One day an Ensign at the Inn
Came down the stairs with rattling din
Upon the porch, where by a rap
He woke a comrade from his nap,
To whom he said: "Come with me, Kean.
And take a stroll around the Green!
"I will!" said Kean, "so soon I can,
To clean my shoes, find boy or man!"

He rang the bell, no servant came;
He rang again; 't was just the same;
The third time came mine host, whose call
Brought Andrew thither from his stall.
Told he should clean the Ensign's shoes,
The boy replied: "Ask what you choose,
And I obey; but this to do
I must refuse, whate'er ensue!"—

"Hear but that youthful rebel, do!"
The irate Ensign called; he drew
His sword and with it cut a whack
Across the daring youngster's back;
He, jumping by one sudden bound
Down from the porch upon the ground,
And stretching forth his hand on high,
Exclaimed, while wildly flashed his eye:

"Through you of all my kin bereft,
An orphan-boy midst strangers left,
Though powerless now, obliged to bear
Your gross abuse, by heav'n I swear:
I shall yet,—yet avenge my wrong,
When grown to manhood, ripe and strong
That men shall tell in years from now:
How Andrew Jackson kept his vow.'"

And as he called so, strong and loud,
He broke athwart the gathered crowd,
And leaving neither clue nor trace,
For ever vanished from the place.
Soon, too, his mem'ry died with all
Who knew him there and heard his call,
Till, after five and thirty years,
It was revived to lips and ears,

When from the Mississippi's mouth
The news was borne through North and South,
How Andrew Jackson there and then
To glorious vict'ry led his men,
And struck the British Lion a blow
That laid his pride for ever low;
And all the world acknowledged now:
That Andrew Jackson kept his vow!

So he avenged his kindred's wrong,
When grown to manhood ripe and strong.
Yet was there not upon his score
Against his foes one grievance more,—
The blow dealt by the Ensign Kean,
Whose boots he had refused to clean?
Yea! and this day brought him as well
Amends for that, as I will tell:

For when the battle's din was hushed
And past the lines, with vict'ry flushed,
The Chieftain rode, he reached a spot,
Where on a stretcher's blood-stained cot
The Britons' second in command
Lay pierced by balls through thigh and hand,
'T was Kean, the Ensign,—General now,
The cause of Andrew Jackson's vow.

Forthwith he had him from the spot
Borne to some safe and sheltering cot,
And bade his surgeon to attend
The wounded, as he would his friend.
Yea! when relieved from duty's care,
Oft as he could, he would repair
To Kean's abode, and with him bide,
And see his every want supplied.

But when, restored from wound and maim,
The Englishman to Jackson came
To thank him for his care once more,
Before he sailed to Albion's shore,—
Then Jackson said to him: "Not I
Deserve your thanks, but God on high,
Who by His Mercy made it true
That I have been *revenged* on you!"

"Revenged, you say? How can this be?"
Then to the Briton's memory
Brought Jackson back that sabre-blow,
Dealt five and thirty years ago,
And added: "Then my boyish will
It was, ill to reward with ill;
I changed my mind since:—anyhow:
Hath Andrew Jackson kept his vow!"

Marion's Grave.*

[Written at Belle Isle, Berkeley County, S. C.]

A SONNET.

HERE dwelt a while, returned from battle's broil,
  In earthly peace the Leader "frank and bold;"
And here he rests beneath his homestead's wold,
In peace eternal after his life's toil.

And here to-day the grateful State whose soil
His labor freed by sacrifice untold,
With homage due restores his tomb of old,
That Time and Elements had made their spoil.

Spare, envious Powers, this emblem of Man's toll
To Marion's worth, paid from their inmost soul,
And keep it sacred, unimpaired and whole;

Yet, if again you must destroy this knoll,
His fame remains,—immortal Song will roll,
As heretofore, his name from pole to pole!

John Laurens, the Bayard of the South.*

A BALMY Southern summer-night
  Hath spread her soothing charms
With an enchantress' magic might
  All o'er the groves and farms
And oozy rice-fields whom beside,
In rambling course, with languid tide,
The Combahee's dark currents glide
  Into the Ocean's arms.

And all is dark, save now and then,
  When lightning rends the gloom,
And o'er the sky with fiery pen
  Writes mystic signs of doom;
And all is silent, save alone
The river's heaving, sullen moan,
And in the pines the nightwind's groan,
  Like voices from the tomb.

*See Notes.

But where the broad plantation-manse
  With whom but few can vie,
Far o'er its acres' broad expanse
  Lords from the bluff on high,
The grounds stand lit with lanterns gay,
The windows shine with candles' ray,
And from its halls sweet minstrel-play
  Floats through the starless sky.

Oft, oft, for festive sport and glee,
  In happy days of yore,
To Beauty and to Chivalry
  This manse had oped its door;
Yet never for as genial cheer
As honored Freedom's champions here,
Come to protect, should foes appear,
  The region 'long the shore.

No doubt, that Mars' resplendent show
  The ladies' hearts endued
With sweet affection's warmest glow,—
  No doubt, that gratitude
For safety from War's threatening storms
Set free their bonds from Fashion's norms,
And Etiquette's stern, rigid forms
  By deeper sway subdued,—

Yet most this charm was due to one
  And to his coming here,
Who had no peer, no paragon
  As perfect cavalier,—
South Carolina's honored son,
The trusty aid of Washington,
Who glory had in battles won
  And in the statesman's sphere,—

JOHN LAURENS, Bayard of the South,
  Well worth the name he bore,
Whose fame was told by every mouth
  From Maine to Georgia's shore;
And as he came by his free will
To shield this neighborhood 'gainst ill,
It was not strange, that he should still
  Be honored all the more.

And as he entered, freedom's gait
  Revealed in every pace,—
And as he stood, high manhood's trait
  Impressed on brow and face,—
And as he spake, his tone and word
Like music by deep feelings stirred,—
And as he danced, light as a bird,
  Embodiment of grace,—

His spirit's deep magnetic charm
  Shed o'er the feast a glow
Of radiant mirth, so weird, so warm,
  None ever felt it so!
And sweeter than the music's swell
The silvery ring of laughter fell,
Like joyous peal of marriage-bell,
  Like glee of endless flow!

But hist! what wily steps without ?
  What rustling in the grass?
It is a spy, a British scout!
  Oh! stop him ere he pass!
He hath marked down your every post;
E'en now his boat glides 'long the coast,
To hither bring the en'my's host!
  Too late! Alas! Alas!

Yet though unseen his shadow melt
  Away in night's dread shroud,
A chill awhile each bosom felt
  Amid that festive crowd.
A pause ensued as through a scare;
Then Laurens, asked to sing an air,
In answer to the Mistress' prayer,
  With courteous homage bowed.

A Moorish ballad 't was he sang,
  From times of Chivalry,
Of passionate love and sabre-clang
  And this refrain for glee:
"For Honor, Freedom, Love, I lie
Smit unto death, yet ere I die,
My last, last thought to thee shall fly !
  Farewell! Remember me!"

Then every heart to woe was moved
  And every eye to tears;
Yet though these thrills far better proved
  Than ghastly, spectral fears,
E'en these he would not long permit
As genii o'er the feast to sit,
And soon won back by lively wit
  The guests to frolic's cheers.

Then from the river rang a shot
  Like leaden die of chance!
The gay assembly heard it not;
  On, laughter went and dance.
Yea! louder, merrier e'en they rose,
As if they meant the hearts to close
'Gainst conscious fears of coming woes
  By pleasure's dizzy trance.

Another shot, another knell!
  Repeated warning's call!
Alike unheard, for revel's spell
  Now reigned supreme o'er all.
E'en Laurens, yielding to its charm,
Once more arose and at his arm
Led forth among the dancers' swarm
  The Mistress of the Hall!

Then, one by one the dancing pairs,
  As if agreed before,
Receded softly to their chairs,
  And left the parlor-floor
Free to the couple, that with grace
Of even motion, blended pace,
With ever more impassioned race,
  In mid-air seemed to soar.

Then, like a stern command of doom,
  That bade them part for aye,
Rang through the night a cannon's boom,
  And had not died away,
When a vedette with furious tramp
Came at full speed across the swamp,
Who called: "The foe attacks our camp!
  Come, come without delay!"

No time to meet for hand or eye!
  No time for parting's plea!
"To arms! To horse!" rang Laurens' cry:
  "Forward!" his next decree!
Yet while he galloped past the Hall,
The valiant knight, ahead of all,
Still waved the falchion with his call:
  "Farewell! Remember me!"

Then o'er the din was Laurens' shout
  Of cheer heard far away,
As from the riverside-redoubt
  He dashed amid the fray,
And charged the foes by bold attack,
And hotly foll'wing in their track,
With power resistless drove them back
  And swept them down the bay.

Once more was heard, yet faint and low,
  —Was space or breeze to blame?—
Brave Laurens' far-off call, as though
  From worlds remote it came.
Now, too, the shots grew few and rare,
But now and then, and here and there,
A dim, dull flash blazed through the air
  Like spark of dying flame.

Then o'er the landscape spread the night
  Again her deepest gloom;
For lightning e'en had ceased to write
  Its mystic signs of doom.
And all was silent, save alone
The river's heaving, sullen moan,
And in the pines the nightwind's groan
  Like voices from the tomb.

At last a far-off drumbeat's stroke
  Relieved the dread suspense;
At last the glare of torches broke
  The darkness, deep and dense.
But why no shout of joyous cheer?
Why that delay in coming here?
Why trails the banner in their rear?
  What is that pageant's sense?

The mournful train hath reached the Hall,
  Within their midst a bier.
None asks: "Who lies beneath that pall?"
  Their sorrow makes it clear:
'T was Laurens, Carolina's son,
The Bayard of the South, who won
Bright fame the battlefield upon
  And in the statesman's sphere.

Alas! for man's uncertain fate!
  Where but one hour ago
His cheerful wit charmed all—in state
  He lies now cold and low!
The flowers, that pleased his eye, now spread
Their fragrance round his funeral-bed;
The lights that beamed on him, now shed
  Upon his bier their glow!

With tears borne to his resting-place,
  A friend spake at his hill:
"Why weep ye? was not bright his race?
  Its ending brighter still?
To vault from love's enraptured dance
At once to death in vict'ry's trance,
What mortal ever had that chance?
  What mortal ever will?"

Low and alone his mound still lies
  Beside the Combahee,
Whose moan, blent with the nightwind's sighs,
  Seems voicing still this plea:
"For Freedom, Honor, Love, I lie
Smit unto death, yet ere I die,
To thee my last, last thought shall fly!
  Farewell! Remember me!"

Osceola's Death.*

ARE the skies to earth descending?
   Will the sea mount up to heaven?
So in mid-air high uniting,
Hold the two their midday-wedding,
Waves and clouds their hands entwining
For their bacchanalean revel
To the music of the tempest's
And the breakers' thunder-voices.
Trembling, quivering, awe-inspired,
Stands the Earth, a speechless witness
To the wildest of all nuptials.

On a mattress, decked with blankets,
Lies in one of Moultrie's casemates
Osceola, patriot, warrior,
Waning,—wasting,—sinking,—dying.
Far from all his kin and brethren,
From his native glades and thickets,
Captive through perfidious treason,
In a narrow cell imprisoned,
Pined away the hero-chieftain.
So, so will the wild-flower wither,
So the royal eagle languish,
Robbed of freedom's vital essence.
In his fever-spell's convulsions
Dreamt the warrior's mind of battle,
And his war-whoop's shout commingled
With the uproar of the cyclone;
Every blast a trumpet-summons,
Every billow's roar an onslaught
On the foe, till weak, exhausted,
Back he sank upon his pillow.

All the while a tender maiden,
Belle, the Warden's only daughter,
Sat beside the sinking hero,
Angel-like his wants attending,—
Smoothing now his ruffled blanket,
Bathing now his feverish temples,
Moistening now his lips with water.
Lone she sat beside the sufferer
In the damp and gloomy casemate
'Gainst whose walls the breakers thundered.
For her sire that morn had early
Rowed across the harbor's waters
To the City for enlisting
Some expert physician's service,
But the cyclone's wrath prevented
His return to Fort and daughter.

* See Notes.

From his fever's dream awakened,
Cast his eyes the Chieftain open,
And with faint voice he inquired
For the sergeant. "I am going."
—Spake he—"to the unknown regions,
Whitherward the spirits' voices
Call me from the tempest's moanings,
From the billows' roaring thunders!"—
"'Tis the voice of God!" the maiden
Interposed with whispered tremor.
"God? Thy God! thou meanest, maiden!
He,—He,—whom thy pale-faced brethren
Call upon midst their injustice,
Midst their breach of faith and promise,
Midst their wrongs that cry to heaven.
His is not the voice that calls me!"—
"Still, 't is He, 't is He, none other!"
Spake with gentle stress the maiden.
"'T is the Father of all creatures,
'Tis the Giver of all blessings,
He who in thy dying hour
Blesses thee, oh Osceola!"—
"Blesses me ? Thou mock'st me, maiden!
"Blesses thee, afore thou diest,
More than e'en thy boldest wishes
Ever dreamt of and desired.
Nobly, grandly thou hast striven
To thy best of understanding,—
Thy first wish thy brethren's welfare,
And thy next thy mem'ry's honor.
Neither, though, by God's wise counsel,
Was fulfilled as thou hadst chosen.
For God's ways are far from ours.
Thy intrepid course continued,
Would have ended in thy brethren's
And with them—thy fame's extinction.
See now, how our Heavenly Father
Leadeth all to far more glorious
End than we ourselves desired.
For what valor's laurels vainly
Strove to win by lifelong labor,
Quick the martyr's thorns accomplish.
Rueful sympathy, awakened
In the bosoms of thy captors
By thy suff'rings' brave endurance,
Will preserve and save thy nation
Through humane and gen'rous treatment,
While, for thee, from out this chamber
Will proceed a brighter halo
Than thy vict'ries ever gave thee.
In thy en'mies' song will flourish
Thy heroic deeds' remembrance
And thy grave thy victors' daughters
Shall—while decking it with flowers,—

Moisten by their tears of sorrow.
Canst thou wish a nobler vengeance?"

"Thanks, my child, I now die happy!
Speak then to Thy Heavenly Father,
That He will receive my Spirit!"
Then in simple, touching manner
Prayed the maiden for the dying,
One hand on his heart, the other
In the Chieftain's pressure resting.
While she prayed, Osceola's spirit
Had departed from his body,
Yet the features of his visage
Bore the stamp of peace and blessing.

But the cyclone had subsided.

Jack.*

[Respectfully dedicated to Mrs. Fanny Perry Beattie.]

IN silence meet, with heads bowed low,
   We have remembered our brave mates,
Who sank beneath the enemy's blow.
   Who since have entered Death's still gates.
Yet one more loss I must proclaim
Of one dear friend of well-known name.
To whom our thoughts with love turn back:
Our Legion's pet,—our gallant *Jack!*

You well remember him, the steed
   Of human sense, of sterling worth,
Well fit, our Legion's barbs to lead,
   As led us men his master forth;
Like him just in the prime of life,
Like him a hero in the strife,
His constant mate in bivouac,
On march and raid,—our gallant *Jack!*

E'en now methinks that I can hear
   His neigh like as a clarion's burst.
The spirit of our beasts to cheer,
   When worn with heat and faint with thirst.
Yet by some spring I see him wait,
Until had drunk his every mate,
Resigned of all alone to lack
The draught's relief—our gallant *Jack!*

But 't was in battle's tumult where
   His spirit most of all would shine!

_____
* See Notes.

How flashed his eye with fiery glare
  When galloping along the line,
Till, when the trumpet's signal blew,
Like as a whirlwind's blast he flew,
And led our Legion's bold attack
Upon the foe,—our gallant *Jack!*

As if his very life were charmed
  From densest fray and battle-smoke
He would emerge unscathed, unharmed
  By bullet or by sabre-stroke.
Not could his master boast such luck,
Who reeled, by fatal missile struck:
Yet safe from capture brought him back
Into our line his gallant *Jack!*

Henceforth, next to our deep regret
  To miss our hero-captain's sight,
Our sorrow was to lose our pet;
  And hence, how great was our delight,
Arrived at home again, to find
How still he kept his war-like mind,
And how drum-roll and rifle-crack
Would still inspire our gallant *Jack!*

So, when Memorial Day arrived
  With its remembrance of the dead
By vet'rans who the fray survived
  And others by like rev'rence led,—
Bedecked with flowers the mounds to grace,
With conscious, rev'rent, solemn pace,
Strode in the sad procession's track
The pet of all, our gallant *Jack!*

For eighteen years he so hath done
  And never missed the sacred rite!
Not so this year! for he is gone
  For evermore from out our sight!
Yet shall we hold his mem'ry dear
As of a friend whom we revere!
So oft our thoughts the Past bring back,
They will recall our gallant *Jack!*

The Two Veterans.

TO the South, to the South, in the season of spring,
  Two Vet'rans were slowly proceeding,
One bearing still shattered his arm in a sling,
  The other's head bandaged and bleeding.

Companions from childhood on neighboring farms
   And welded by friendship enraptured,
They fought for their country as comrades-in-arms,
   Were wounded together and captured.

In a hospital-ward of a Northern State
   There bedded like brother by brother,
The comrades lay calmly resigned to their fate,
   Still thankful to comfort each other

By hopeful assurance, by counsels of cheer,
   Each feigning his best not to doubt them,
Though knowing full well, that their wounds were severe,
   And the typhus was rampant about them,—

The typhus, the Fury, that strides in the wake
   Of War with the steps of hyenas,
That stalks through his camp-grounds, but loveth to make
   The sick-wards her horrors' arenas.

So, patients and captives, with the sights of disease
   And contagion in hourly communion,
They quickly departed the moment when peace
   Again was restored in the Union,

Unheeding their comrades', their doctors' advice,
   Self-aware of their wounded condition,
They recked it but little, when liberty's prize
   So temptingly stood 'fore their vision,—

Once more to be free, like a bird in the sky,
   Untrammeled, unfettered, unhindered,
And willed it God's mercy, to die, yea! to die
   At their Southern home 'mong their kindred.

Through the South, through the South, in the season of spring.
   The Vet'rans were slowly proceeding,
One bearing still shattered his arm in a sling,
   The other's head bandaged and bleeding.

So onward they struggled from sunrise till late,
   O'er mountains and valleys and canyons,
From City to City, through County and State,
   With hunger and thirst for companions,—

Each footstep, each movement a current of pain,
   That shot through their bodies intensely,
Each windgust, each hailstorm, each downpour of rain
   Augmenting their suff'rings immensely.

Though often exhausted they sank by the road,
  Yet onward and onward they wandered,
Till they came to the vale where the Broad, where the Broad,
  The stream of their childhood, meandered.

"O'er the hill-top, the hill-top, at length, at length,
  Lies the Mecca, for which we contended!
Have courage, my brother, and summon thy strength!
  Our journey, our sufferings are ended!"

Up the hill-side, the hill-side the veterans strode
  With footsteps so painful, so weary;
Yet steep though the slope was and rugged the road,
  With bosoms, with faces so cheery.

On the hill-top, the hill-top the veterans stood,
  The valley lay open before them!
What terror unspeakable ices their blood?
  What tremors and shudders come o'er them?

Near the Broad, near the Broad, where in times gone by
  Their homesteads so friendly were standing,
Two chimneys were rearing their ruins on high,
  Heav'n's wrath on the plund'rers demanding,—

Two chimneys, all blackened by soot and by smoke,
  Two places, quite empty around them;
The stories of horror, of anguish, they spoke,
  What mortal would venture to sound them?

Like as hit by a ball in the heat of the fight,
  Like as smit by a thunderbolt's violence,
So the comrades were struck by the terrible sight
  And sank by the road-side in silence.

So motionless, speechless and torpid they lay,
  Their souls' and their bodies' wounds burning,
Till the tears to their eyelids found back their way,
  And words to their lips were returning:

" 'T is over, all over, my brother, my friend!
  How tragic our drama's conclusion!
Oh! would that in mercy heav'n spared us this end,
  This wakening from blissful illusion!

"A power steals o'er me like the shades of the night,
  Defeating my strongest endeavor,
And seizing my senses with forcible might:
  Farewell then, my comrade, for ever!"

For a moment aroused, as from slumber's deep sway,
  The other clasped warmly his brother;
So friendly, so fondly the veterans lay
  Unconscious aside of each other.

———

Just then from the bushes, first far, then near,
  Rang the voices of children united:
"Oh mamma! oh auntie! what berries stand here!
  So many we nowhere have sighted!"

Yet presently summoned quite diff'rent a call,
  Surprisal and anguish implying,
With the uttermost hurry the gatherers all
  To the place where the comrades were lying.

"'T is my husband! 'T is father!" so echoed their cries
  Of despair when they failed to arouse them;
But quickly recov'ring, they began to devise
  Strong means how to save and to house them.

Long, long hung the veterans' lives by a hair,
  Long, long stood Death's shadows cast o'er them,
But loving attendance, solicitous care
  Succeeded at last to restore them.

For the first time they learned then how neighborly aid
  New homes for the suff'rers had founded,
Out of sight from the hill, in the midst of a glade,
  By a forest's dark shadows surrounded.

In the South, in the South, in the front of their cot,
  Two vet'rans are sitting at even,
Amidst their beloved, content with their lot,
  And praising the mercy of heaven!

——— ⚜ ———

The Heroes of the Charleston Earthquake.*

[Respectfully dedicated to Mrs. F. S. Rodgers.]

'TIS night! The City by the Sea
  Lies tranquil, wrapt in slumber!
And why should sleep her eyelids flee
  Or fear her rest encumber?
Hath God not been her guard and guide,
And through the Past stood at her side?
What ills then need she dread that hide
  Beneath Night's shades of umber?

* See Notes.

And with her fear of God, she keeps
   Her household well in order;
Her law's stern eye that never sleeps,
   Checks crime and all disorder.
The flame, her foe in times of yore,
No longer feeds upon her store;
Harmless the tides surge 'round her door
   Peace dwells within her border.

And so she rests in sleep profound,
   Refreshed again to waken!
When she is roused as at a bound,—
   Her very ground is shaken!
Like houses built of card-board, so
Her homes, her spires, rock to and fro!
Her walls áre laid like forests low,
   When by a storm o'ertaken!

Then from five thousand pleasant homes,
   Now creaking, crashing, bending,
From fifty thousand bosoms comes
   One cry, one wail ascending
To heaven on high with one accord.
Couched in that deep-despairing word:
"Oh save us, save thy people, Lord!
   From death o'er them impending!"

From swaying, tottering buildings then
   Rush forth in wild confusion
The people,—children, women, men,—
   With but one resolution:
To gain the free, the outer air,
To reach some open plot or square,
Away from walls, whose shelt'ring care
   Hath proved a dire illusion!

So 'mid the dark of that dread night
   In groups together banding.
The people stand bereft of light;
   But hail! a glare expanding,
As of the moon, now spreads a glow;
Alas! 't is fire! another woe!
Arisen to lay the houses low,
   That earthquake shocks left standing.

Haste, firemen, to the rescue haste,
   And stop the flames' contagion!
How can they come, when flat and waste
   Is laid their every station?
When o'er the wires that prostrate lie,
No signal's call to them can fly.
When rubbish-piles fill mountain high
   The streets with desolation?

Another shock, another cry
  From livid, trembling faces!
And brighter stream the flames on high
  From half a dozen places!
Ah! glorious City by the Sea!
Thy fate seems sealed by Heaven's decree!
When morn shall dawn, nought but debris
  Will mark thy site, thy traces!

Hark! o'er the roar of fiery tongues,
  Of walls and mortar crumbling,
Comes a familiar ring of gongs,
  A well-known sound of rumbling!
It rids the hearts from wan despair,
Relieves them of their direst care
And e'en sets lips, unused to prayer,
  To fervent, thankful mumbling.

It is the bold, it is the brave,
  Who come without persuasion
On ev'ry side, the town to save
  From utter conflagration.
Another shock! the horses rear,
And stand stock-still like trembling deer,—
Yet human arms, unbent by fear,
  Replace them in their station.

And so o'er hills of brick and sand
  O'er prostrate poles and wire,
They drag the engines by the hand
  To hydrants near the fire.
Though 'neath them rocks the earth with fright,
They cease not in their gallant fight,
Till they have tamed the element's might
  And quenched its ruthless ire!

Saved was the City by the Sea,
  And soon by own endeavor
And friendly aid rose from debris,
  Fair, young and strong and clever.
Yet will the mem'ry of the brave
Who risked their limbs and lives to save
The city from her peril grave,
  Abide with her for ever!

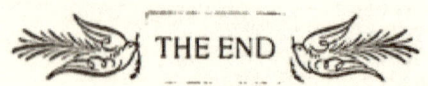

THE END

NOTES.

NOTES.

The Bell of Dorchester. (Page 15.)

In 1696 a Colony of Congregationalists, from Dorchester, in Massachusetts, ascended the Ashley River, near to its head, and there founded a town to which they gave the name of that which they had left. Dorchester became a town of some importance, having a moderately large population and considerable trade. It is now deserted; the habitations and inhabitants have alike vanished; but the reverend spire, rising through the forest trees which surround it, still attests the place of their worship and where so many of them yet repose.—*Wm. Gilmore Simms: History of South Carolina, page 52.*

The Old Fort of Dorchester is situated on a bend of the Ashley, and is built so as to command both the ascent and descent of the river. It is in a remarkable state of preservation. The walls are very thick and solid, and are made of a composition of oyster shells and cement. * * * In the centre of the enclosure a mound of rubbish marks the site of the magazine. * * * This fort was often used during the Revolution, being held alternately by the British and by the Americans. In 1775 a general order was issued by General Moultrie to re-inforce the garrison. The order was addressed to "Capt. Francis Marion."—*J. I. W. in the Charleston Sunday News, November 17, 1895.*

The Legend of the Rice Plant. (Page 21.)

The cultivation of rice was first commenced in South Carolina in 1694. A vessel from Madagascar in distress, put into Charleston Harbor, the captain of which had some previous acquaintance with Landgrave Thomas Smith, to whom he gave a small parcel of rough rice which was in the cook's bag on board; this Mr. Smith planted in a moist spot in his garden (now Longitude Alley, in the City of Charleston). The proceeds he distributed among his friends, and in a few years after, rice became one of the staple productions of the Colony.—*Ramsay's History of South Carolina.*

A brigantine from Madagascar put into the Colony and gave some seed rice to Mr. Woodward, which, in a few years, was dispersed through the Colony.—*Carroll's Historical Collections of South Carolina.*

Cateechee, the Indian Maiden. (Page 24.)

Fort Ninety-Six, established by the British about the year 1750, near the Town of Cambridge, and so called, because it was 96 miles distant from Fort Prince George, on the Keowee

River, became during the Revolutionary War the most important stronghold of the British in the up-country. A pine grove now covers its walls and interior, the dimensions of which are sufficient proofs of its considerable size. The entrance to the mine, constructed by Kosciusco, Gen. Greene's engineer during the siege of the Fort in 1781, is visible to this day.

THE LEGEND OF STONY BATTER. (Page 26.)

Stony Batter is a hamlet in the southeastern part of Newberry County, near the Town of Prosperity. It is still inhabited by the descendants of that thrifty race, the German Palatines, who settled it about 1730.

THE LEGEND OF ALTAMONT. (Page 28.)

The outline of the western crest of Paris Mountain, in the County of Greenville, reveals the contours of a giant lying flat upon the surface of the plain.

THE LEGEND OF THE WHITE HORSE ROAD. (Page 35.)

This road extends from north to south through almost the entire length of Greenville County.

THE LEGEND OF CÆSAR'S HEAD. (Page 38.)

This highest and most picturesque summit of the Blue Ridge in South Carolina received its name from the resemblance of a huge cliff, jutting out from the peak, to the profile of Julius Cæsar's countenance.

THE PRIZE CONTEST OF THE THIRTEEN. (Page 53.)

Amidst the general desolation, the women of Carolina exhibited an example of more than masculine fortitude. They displayed so ardent, so rare a love of country, that scarcely could there be found in ancient or modern history an instance more worthy to excite surprise and admiration. * * * To this heroism of the women of Carolina, it is principally to be imputed, that the love and even the name of liberty, were not totally extinguished in the Southern Provinces.— *Charles Botta's History of the War of the Independence of the United States of America, Book XIII, pages 261 and 262.*

Such, throughout the dreary War of the Revolution, was universally the character of the Carolina women. The sons fought, but who shall measure the aid and comfort and influence which the daughters brought to the conflict? This will need a volume to itself.— *Wm. Gilmore Simms' History of South Carolina, page 308.*

Among the numbers who were banished from their families and whose property was seized by the conquerors, many examples could be produced of ladies cheerfully parting with their sons, husbands and brothers, exhorting them to fortitude and perseverance, and repeatedly entreating them never to suffer family attachments to interfere with the duty they owed to their country. When, in the progress of the war, they were also comprehended under a general sentence of banishment, with equal resolution they parted with their native country and the many endearments of home,—followed their husbands into prison-ships and distant lands, where, though they had long been in the habit of giving, they were reduced to the necessity of receiving charity.—*Ramsay's History of South Carolina, page 198.*

MARIAN GIBBES. (Page 55.)

The incident described here occurred in 1779, when the British General Prevost, setting out from Savannah, made an unsuccessful attempt to surprise Charles Town.

REBECCA MOTTE. (Page 57.)

Fort Motte lies above the fork on the south side of the Congaree. The works of the British were built around the mansion house of the lady whose name it bore, and from which British recklessness had expelled her. Under these circumstances, Mrs. Motte, who had been driven for shelter to a neighboring hovel, produced an Indian bow, which, with a quiver of arrows, she presented to the American commander, "Take these," she said, "and expel the enemy. These will enable you to fire the house." Her earnest entreaty at last prevailed with the reluctant Marion. Combustibles were fastened to the arrows, which were shot into the roof of the dwelling, and the patriotic woman rejoiced in the destruction of her property when it secured the conquest of her countrymen.—*Wm. Gilmore Simms' History of South Carolina, page 308.*

LOVE WILL ABIDE. (Page 73.)

This story (with names changed) has been gleaned from the "Annals of Newberry, by Judge O'Neal." The Dead Line extended along what is now called the Ridge Road in the so-named Dutch Forks, lying between the Broad and Saluda Rivers.

EMILY GEIGER'S RIDE. (Page 78.)

Emily Geiger, after the war, was married to Colonel Threewits, a rich planter on the Congaree. She was buried in the old Threewits burying ground, in Lexington County, ten miles from Columbia.   It has been suggested, that her likeness be used in the revised copy of the coat-of-arms of the State of South Carolina, which is soon to be prepared.—*Report of the Exercises of Peabody Memorial Day, May 12, 1893, by D. B. Johnson, President of Winthrop Normal College.*

KATE FOWLER.   (Page 81.)

A woman was the instrument employed by the British for encouraging Cruger to protract the siege.   Residing in the neighborhood, she had visited the camp of Greene, under some pretense of little moment.   The daughter of one tried patriot and the sister of another, she had been received at the General's table and permitted the freedom of the encampment. But she had formed a matrimonial engagement with a British officer, and the ties of love had proved stronger than those of any other relationship.   In the opportunities thus afforded to her, she contrived to apprise the garrison, that she had a communication from Lord Rawdon.—*Wm. Gilmore Simms' History of South Carolina, p. 314.*

The creek that flows down from the Old Fort of Ninety-Six into the Saluda, still bears the name of Kate Fowler's Branch.

THE HEROINES OF CASTLE PINCKNEY.   (Page 83.)

On August 21, 1888, Castle Pinckney, situated upon a shoal in Charleston Harbor, was the scene of the heroic rescue of capsized fishermen by Mrs. Mary Whiteley and her daughter Miss Maud King, the latter at that time no more than thirteen years old.   The United States Government duly honored their brave deed by conferring upon them gold medals in appreciation of their heroism.

MARION'S LEAP.   (Page 94.)

The incident narrated here occurred in March, 1780, at the house of Mr. Alexander McQueen, in Tradd Street, Charles Town.

SONG OF MARION'S RANGERS.   (Page 96.)

This poem as well as that of "Isaac Hayne," page 90, together with several others contained in this collection, has been set to music, in which form they may appear hereafter.

ANDREW JACKSON.   (Page 99.)

In one of his State papers President Jackson says that South Carolina is his native State.   Mrs. Stinson also told me that he was born in South Carolina.   But Parton shows very clearly that the house in which General Jackson was born, stood a few yards beyond the South Carolina line, and in North Carolina. * * * The Waxhaw Settlement, however, was in South Carolina, where he went to school and attended church. * * * —*Reminiscences of Public Men by Ex-Gov. B. F. Perry, p. 30.*

MARION'S GRAVE·AT BELLE ISLE. (Page 102.)

On the 27th of February, 1795, General Francis Marion died at his plantation, Belle Isle, St. John's Parish, and there he lies buried. His grave was marked by a marble slab, bearing a suitable inscription, which however was subsequently shattered by a sycamore tree that had fallen upon it. In this condition it lay for a long time, until in 1892 the State Legislature appropriated a moderate fund for the restoration of his grave-monument, which was unveiled with appropriate ceremonies in April, 1893.

JOHN LAURENS, THE BAYARD OF THE SOUTH. (Page 102.)

At the place of Mrs. Stock, Laurens spent the night in the enjoyment of company, and in the utterance of feelings and sentiments which heighten the melancholy interest of the fatal event which closed his adventure. The warm hospitality of the lady of the mansion, and the blandishments of female society, beguiled the time, and the company did not separate until two hours before the time when the detachment was set into motion. * * * The enemy had probably received some intelligence of the march of the detachment, and landing on the north bank of the river, had formed an ambuscade in a place covered with fennel and high grass. Laurens fell at the first fire.— *Wm. Gilmore Simms' History of South Carolina, p. 380.*

OSCEOLA'S DEATH. (Page 107.)

Osceola, the Seminole Chief, had been invited to a parley by General Jessup, and treacherously been made a prisoner. He was confined in Fort Moultrie, where he died soon after his incarceration. His grave lies outside of the Fort and is marked by a slab bearing the words: "Here lies Osceola, Patriot, Warrior: Died February 20, 1838."

JACK. (Page 109.)

Jack was the favorite horse of Colonel Beattie of Greenville, and faithfully bore his master, Captain in the Hampton Legion, during the campaign in Virginia, 1861–1863. After Colonel Beattie's disablement by wounds, the horse returned with his master to Greenville, where it became the idol of the family, as well as of the people of the city, and where it, especially on Memorial Day, participated in the parades and patriotic exhibitions of the city. It died at the age of 28 years, A. D. 1883.

THE HEROES OF THE CHARLESTON EARTHQUAKE. (Page 113.)

During the past year, in the sudden emergency of the earthquake, the whole Fire Department of the city was brought to a test as to discipline and courage which has never been equaled by any Fire Department in the history of this country.

A few minutes after the disastrous earthquake shocks, fires were discovered in several different quarters of the city; the fire alarm had been rendered useless, several of the engine houses were themselves obstructed by debris from their own fallen walls; an entire community was in the confusion incident to a sudden calamity,—and yet, amid all these disabilities, the firemen displayed their devotion to duty, and amidst crumbling walls and buildings, and entangling wires obstructing the streets, moved their apparatus to the several scenes of conflagration, and carrying their hose by hand over ground so obstructed, and still trembling under earthquake shocks, by their supreme efforts saved the city from further disastrous destruction by fire.—*Report by Firemaster F. S. Rodgers, Esq., in Mayor Courtenay's Year Book of 1886.*

www.ingramcontent.com/pod-product-compliance
Lightning Source LLC
Chambersburg PA
CBHW031928060726
47496CB00008BA/2424